THE TRAVELLING MENACE

by

John Fullick

This special limited edition first published in Dolton, Devon by
Yolande Ifold, July 2019

Text copyright © John Fullick
Cover photographs copyright © David Ifold

John Fullick asserts the moral right to be identified as the author
of this work

ISBN 978-1-09-383555-7

Published in Great Britain by Kindle Direct Publishing

Private limited edition; not currently available for general sale.

CONTENTS

Acknowledgements

Thank you to anyone who has contributed in any way. Special thanks go to Paul Donovan and Alan Haynes who helped me (the Editor) unstintingly. I am grateful for their time, professional help and advice. Thanks also to my husband, David Ifold, for the image of the author and the front cover.

Yolande Ifold

Editor's Foreword

John and his husband, Tony, and I have been close friends for a long time. A number of years ago, during a long journey transporting horses to a dressage competition, John confided in me that he had written a story for young people about young people who possessed extraordinary abilities. His wish was that, one day, he might see it in print. John later provided me with a copy of what he had written in the hope that I might edit his manuscript and help him take it further as he didn't know how to proceed.

At that time I also knew next to nothing about printing and publishing and how to have a manuscript accepted by a publishing house. Self-publishing then was a relatively new (and somewhat frowned on) concept. I duly started editing, somewhat at a loss and the years passed by without anything being accomplished as there were horses to ride, stables to clean and competitions to enter.

Last autumn (2018), I suddenly woke to the idea as to what could be a better way of repaying John for all his kindness to me than handing him an actual copy of his book, *The Travelling Menace.*

So with the incredibly generous help, support and expertise of two friends, Paul Donovan (a former *Sunday Times* columnist and commissioned author of four books) and Alan Haynes (a former printer and publisher, and enthusiastic yachtsman), serious editing, proof reading and research into ways of printing and publishing, formatting and creating page layout and cover design has been undertaken by the three of us over many months in top secret over numerous glasses of ginger beer. It has been a most enjoyable challenge and a huge learning curve.

The final result is this special limited edition publication of *The Travelling Menace* for a highly thought of, very respected and loved member of our community and dear friend to many.

Happy 50th Birthday John.

Yolande Ifold (Editor)
2019

gargoyle

noun

noun: gargoyle; plural noun: gargoyles

a grotesque carved human or animal face or figure projecting from the gutter of a building, typically acting as a spout to carry water clear of a wall.

Origin

Middle English: from Old French gargouille 'throat', also 'gargoyle' (because of the water passing through the throat and mouth of the figure); related to Greek gargarizein 'to gargle' (imitating the sounds made in the throat).

Chapter 1

THE NOT SO ORDINARY FAMILY

It was the last week of the summer holidays. David sat in the window watching the rain. It was that really wet rain. You know the sort? If you stood out in it for just one minute you would be soaked right through. However, unlike most boys of his age, instead of moaning or feeling down about it, David simply thought how lovely it would be tomorrow when the sun came out. David didn't hope that the sun would shine the next day, he knew it would.

Ever since he was a small boy, David was able to sense when good things were going to happen and for many years it had been just that - a feeling. But as he got older, he gradually became more aware of details (what feeling good was about, or where, or who it was coming from). David had never discussed this ability with anyone. Sometimes he had unwittingly voiced his feelings about something only to be met with some very strange comments or looks. The only person who never seemed fazed about it was his grandmother, Edna. She never dismissed what he said but she never drew attention to it either. She simply reassured him that he had a special gift and said no more.

David lived with his family (mum, dad, older sister Jessica, and baby brother Joe) at 5 Buemont Road, Braunton, Devon in a modern semi-detached house in a quiet part of town. From the outside it looked like all the others - a sad soulless little box. However, because of the people who lived there, Number 5 was very different! To most people, the Trents seemed like a normal family. Mr Mathew Trent was a tall, slim man with long wavy blonde hair. He had a relaxed attitude to parenting and never said things like "Have you done your homework?" or "Is it time for bed yet?" He ran a small arts and crafts shop in the town. Mrs Jill Trent was a short, slender lady also with long blonde hair but hers was straight and usually tied back in a pony tail. She had worked as a personal assistant for a local businessman for several years but had given up this position before Joe was born. However, although Mrs Trent was always busy caring for the family, she was never too busy to listen to other people's worries and always offered a shoulder to cry on.

Jessica, the oldest of the Trent children was, at fourteen, very pretty with blonde hair and light green eyes (David had noticed, though, that her eye colour seemed to darken to a deep emerald when she was upset). Much to everyone's surprise, she had decided, just recently, to become a goth and had had her hair dyed black and wore black makeup - all of which seemed to match her dark mood of late. Joe was the youngest. Since his arrival two years ago, the whole family seemed to spend more time together. Like his sister and brother, David had fair hair. He was taller than most boys of twelve. His eyes were blue and his warm disposition meant that people were instantly drawn to him. Strangely, although the children at his school liked to talk to and be near David, he currently had no really close friends, no one to confide in, no one to be close to. However, although none of the family members realised it yet, life in the Trent household was about to change unexpectedly.

"Bring! Bring! Bring! Bring!" the telephone rang.

Mrs Trent, being the nearest, picked it up. "Braunton three eight two," she stated.

Luckily there was a chair next to the telephone because what Mrs Trent was told, by the police officer at the other end of the line, made her feel unsteady on her feet. She sank gasping for breath into the chair. After a few moments she managed to compose herself and take in the information the police officer was giving her. After thanking the police officer, Mrs Trent replaced the receiver only to pick it up again and dial the number of Mr Trent's shop.

"Mathew!" she shouted down the phone as the receiver was picked up at the other end. "You must come home Mathew. It's mother! Something very strange has happened."

"Calm down Jill," soothed Mr Trent. "Calm down and tell me what has happened."

"It's Mum," sobbed Mrs Trent. "The police have rung! They said that she had been found wandering around in Hyde Park in London. They said that she seems really confused. She cannot remember who she is or what she was doing there."

"Right," said Mr Trent. "Just let me shut up the shop and I will be straight home."

No sooner had her mother replaced the phone, Jessica came bursting in the front door and taking one look at her mother's pale face demanded to know what was the matter - what was wrong. Mrs Trent calmed Jessica down and explained what had happened.

The police arranged for someone to escort Gran as far as

the local railway station and several hours later the whole family was waiting on the platform to meet her.

"I just can't believe it," said Mrs Trent. "When I took my mother to the station the day before yesterday for her trip to London she seemed fine. We chatted normally and she told me she was looking forward to seeing her old school friend."

The train pulled into the station. When the throng of people had passed, there she was, being helped along the platform by a young policewoman. However, instead of the bright happy face they all knew, they were met by a blank stare. The policewoman explained that they had no real idea what had happened but the old lady seemed very distressed and confused. The police had been able to identify her only by the bus pass in her handbag.

Once at home, Gran seemed to brighten and was quite content to sit in the chair next to Joe's playpen. Mrs Trent decided that they should have a family meeting and called everyone into the kitchen. David was the last to arrive from upstairs. When they were all seated at the kitchen table, Mrs Trent suggested that as Gran was not herself she should stay with them for a while. This would mean, however, that someone would have to give up their bedroom.

David had already anticipated this situation. He said, "That's okay. I have just finished moving my stuff. I am quite happy to share with Joe." There was a pause.

"That's so sweet of you," said Mrs Trent, breaking the awkward silence. As she turned away, David saw a tear run down her face.

The next few days flew by. There was very little improvement in Gran's condition but she seemed quite content just to be surrounded by her family. Dr Ward called in most days. He had known Edna for many years and although he found it hard to believe, he had diagnosed Alzheimer's disease or "Old Timer's" as Mrs Trent preferred to call Gran's condition.

The sun continued to shine like nothing had happened. How could something so life-changing occur and the outside world just carry on as normal? The weekend was spent getting organised for the new school year. There were new uniforms to buy; books, bags and sports kit to find. Mr Trent, after long discussion with the doctor and Gran's lawyer, decided that Wheelwright Cottage (Gran's home) should be sold as she was going to need full-time care while she continued to live with them.

Mrs Trent had placed an advertisement in the local paper saying, *"Wanted. Kind, caring person to help look after a young child and elderly grandma."* She had hoped to go back to work, now that Joe was old enough, but her plans would have to wait until someone was found.

Chapter 2

THE PAST AND THE FUTURE

Three weeks passed. The two oldest Trent children settled back at school as if nothing had happened. There had been no replies to Mrs Trent's advertisement so she put her search for a new job on hold. There was also no success in selling Wheelwright Cottage. Plenty of people had wanted to look around the property, but all had left in a hurry saying that there was something very strange about the house – something that made them feel unwelcome and uncomfortable.

"I can't believe it", stated Mr Trent. "The house always seems so welcoming to me."

"Well, you know what old houses are like, dear, when they have been empty for a while", reassured his wife. "It probably just needs a good airing."

So on that note, Mr and Mrs Trent decided that they would go there the following weekend and sort the place out.

For David, being back at school was difficult. As much as he liked the company of his fellow pupils, he found it very hard to concentrate (the teachers had been commenting that his work was suffering due to his lack of focus). David's ability to sense people's positive thoughts was very distracting as he had no control over what he was experiencing and was constantly being bombarded with images. Also he was never sure whether what he was feeling was in the present or something that was going to happen in the future. He was told off, many times, for looking into space when he was picturing someone's happy thoughts. When David returned home from school that Friday afternoon, he thought how much he was looking forward to the trip to Gran's house. He had enjoyed many happy holidays there when he was younger.

Two hours later the whole family was packed and ready to go. They all squeezed into the family car and off they went. Mrs Trent had explained to her mother where they were going but if she understood she had made no sign at all. Gran had barely spoken since they had collected her from the railway station but seemed most content just to sit and watch the rest of the family go about their day. She was happiest when Joe was around - she smiled and there even seemed to be a sparkle in her eyes.

It did not take long to get to their destination as Lower Hamdon was only ten miles from Braunton. As they approached the village the roads narrowed. The lane leading from the village to Wheelwright Cottage even had grass growing down the middle of it. They pulled up outside the garden gate where the For Sale sign had been erected. The sun was shining and David thought that the cottage looked just how he remembered it. But, as the Trents made their way up the garden path, passing the two very ugly gargoyles that sat on the gate posts, they could see that there was a look of neglect about the place. Gran had always kept the garden very tidy, the windows clean and never left empty milk bottles on the step. Mr Trent rummaged in his pockets for the large old fashioned key that opened the studded oak front door. The key clonked in the lock and after a strong push the door opened with a loud groan.

As they walked into the large hallway, they were hit by the slightly damp musty smell of a house that had not been lived in for some time. Mrs Trent sent Jessica and David upstairs to open all the windows. David knew the house so well; he had spent many long afternoons exploring everywhere when he was younger. He went straight to the room in which he had always slept when staying with his gran. As he walked through the door David was aware of a feeling of home, not just because he had spent time here, but because he could picture all his family here. It felt strange - like living in a parallel world. Looking around he could visualise all their possessions and sensed an awareness of their future life here. His gifts were expanding. He had never before experienced such a clear vision involving so many people.

"When we live here, I would like the front bedroom, overlooking the lane. If that's okay with you?" David asked his mother when he returned downstairs.

His mother looked at him and smiled. "What makes you think we are going to live here?" she asked.

David looked back at her. He had spoken without thinking. "It just makes sense to me," he muttered. "And I'm sure that Gran would be happier here." He turned and walked into the garden telling himself that he would have to be more careful in the future not to speak his thoughts out loud.

After walking the perimeter of the garden, David came across the old apple tree growing in the front garden next to the road. It had fallen over and crashed through the hedge bordering the lane. Although someone had cut back the branches that had landed in the road the bulk of it was still there, so David set out to tell his dad about it. He found his father sitting in the kitchen talking to his mother. His gran was watching Joe play with his favourite toy, a small brown teddy, which looked a bit worn around the edges. Everywhere Joe went, Teddy had to go too.

"Where is Jessica?" asked David.

"I think she is still upstairs", replied his mother.

So David headed back up the stairs wondering where she might be. He looked in all the bedrooms. When there was only one left, he opened the door of his grandmother's bedroom. Jessica was sitting on the bed holding a small wooden box. As he moved closer David recognised the carving on the top of the box. It was the one that they had been allowed to play with as children. Inside the box were many precious and semi-precious gemstones. Their grandmother used to ask them to choose one and would tell them that for every stone there was a story. Jessica had not even looked up when David entered the room, but now he could see that she was crying.

"Don't cry," he whispered. "We have had happy times

and Gran is still with us."

When Jessica spoke her voice trembled. "She is not the same, though, is she?"

As David looked at his sister he was once again reminded of a conversation he had had with his grandmother. Growing up, he had always seen people not just as individuals but as colours. He could see the colours that surrounded each person - some were bright, others pale, but only Jessica's seemed to have a dark rim on the outside. Other people's colours just seemed to blur around the edges. So once when he was alone with his grandmother, he asked her about it.

"Well my dear," she had said. "What you are seeing are people's auras – this is the light that everybody gives off." David explained about his sister's aura. His gran had looked thoughtful for a moment and then said, "I think it is because she is trying to disguise her aura so as not to let other people see the real her." That was all she had said at the time and David had not pushed for more information but had just accepted what he had been told. He had always taken it for granted that his gran would be around to ask about these things; so now he felt alone with his thoughts and unanswered questions.

"I am going to take these with me," Jessica said in a low voice. "Perhaps they might help her to remember." She picked up the box and walked out of the room.

David stayed sitting on the bed remembering the stories his gran had told them. There had been so many and they all came back to him as he looked at each stone in turn. His favourite story was the one connected with the rose quartz piece which was a beautiful pink colour. Gran had described a woman who many years ago had been born with the gift of looking into other people's souls and being able to tell if they were good or bad. She had dedicated her life to helping other people see the right path ahead and guided them gently to a future filled with happiness. This woman met a man who she immediately knew would be her life partner. They married and had a daughter. When war began, her husband was called up to join the army. The day his call-up documents arrived she sensed that he was not destined to return to her. In her distress, she sought answers from the stones that she had used to help others and after some time, she discovered that amber (although not actually a stone but fossilised resin from prehistoric tree sap) had protective properties. So on the day he was due to leave, she gave her husband a ring with amber set into it.

"Promise me, that you will never take this off," she begged him.

As he placed it on his finger she felt his future change. She visualised him returning home to her and so he did. Three times he was called away and three times he returned. The fourth time, she waved him off at the station, without a care in the world as she was sure her husband would soon be home. However, within days of his departure she started having terrible dreams that something had happened and she would never see him again. Eventually a letter arrived from her husband saying that he was being sent abroad, that he had been ill and had lost a lot of weight so he was sending her the ring for safe keeping, as it had become too loose and he was afraid that he would lose it. By the time she had finished reading the letter, she knew that he would never return. So when the army contacted her to say her husband was missing in action, she could sense that he was already dead. The woman raised her daughter alone, never looking for another partner, as she felt that she would not be able to cope if she were to lose someone else. She also never told her daughter of her psychic abilities, hoping that she might spare her daughter some of the hurt she had experienced.

David came out of his trance-like state to hear his mother calling, saying it was time to go.

"Shut the windows on the way down, there's a good boy."

Chapter 3

A NEW HOME AND A NEW FRIEND

A couple of days had passed before the talk that David knew was coming took place. His parents called them all into the sitting room and once they were sitting down, their father began. "Your mother and I have been talking. We think it might be a good idea if you all agree, of course, that we should move into Gran's cottage."

David caught his mother's eye. She gave him a little wink. "Since we have not been able to sell the cottage we think, that is your mother and I, that the cottage would give us more room. It has been in the family for so long it might be the perfect home for us to grow as a family. Also your gran might be happier in her own home."

Jessica needed no encouragement. She said that she had no objections as it would not even mean a change of school for her, just a longer bus journey. After the family meeting was over and they had all agreed it was the right idea, David returned to his room. Although he was looking forward to moving to Wheelwright Cottage, it would mean a change of school for him. Although it was fair to say that he had no close friends, he would miss the life that he had grown up with. But the lure of the bright future he could see made him smile.

Things seemed to move very quickly after that. The very day their house in Braunton had gone on the market, they had an offer for the asking price and the buyer wanted to move in as quickly as possible. Soon the whole family was involved in packing, cleaning and generally clearing out the rubbish that they had collected over the years. Before long it was the day of the move. The removal men arrived at eight thirty in the morning and after endless cups of tea, the van was full. Once again they all squashed into the family car. This time the trip seemed to take forever. All the family were so keen to start this new adventure. They arrived at the house in plenty of time so as to be able to open everything up, before the removal lorry arrived. Mr Trent had been quite firm with them about how much they could bring as Gran's house was already furnished and full of her own possessions. Even so, as the endless stream of boxes and furniture was brought into the house, it was obvious that there was not going to be enough room for it all.

"Never mind!" Mrs Trent kept saying. "There will be time to sort through everything later, let's just get it all in and unpack the essentials."

David had already planned where everything would go in his new room, so it hardly took him any time at all. When he had finished he went downstairs to see if he could be of any help to his mum and dad. Mr Trent, in his usual style, was wandering around in the sitting room, trying to see where there might be a space for the things that they had brought. He did not even seem to notice David standing in the doorway, so David decided that he was best left and carried on to the kitchen. He found his mother was rearranging pots and pans into various cupboards. She looked up as he walked into the room.

"Put the kettle on for me," said his mother. "There's a good boy."

That evening, after dinner, the whole family were relaxing in the sitting room. Dad had managed to light a fire, which was filling the whole room with a warm glow. David sat on the floor watching the yellow and red flames dancing in the hearth. He looked around at the rest of the family. In some ways it seemed that they looked more at home here than he remembered in their previous house. Jessica was reading a book. Mrs Trent was watching a documentary about Native American Indians and Mr Trent, glasses slipping down his nose, was snoring very loudly. The only person who met his gaze was his grandmother. Instead of the normal blank stare, there seemed to be a sparkle in her eyes or was it just the reflection of the dancing flames?

David shuffled across the floor to sit next to Gran's chair. He put his hand on her hand. She was holding something. As he took it he heard her say quietly, "It's for you."

On closer inspection, he saw it was a gold chain with a pale blue sapphire pendant. As he held it in the palm of his hand he could have sworn that it was glowing as if there was a light inside it.

He heard a whisper. "Promise me you will never be without it."

But as David turned to speak to Gran he was met with a blank stare. If he had not been holding the pendant in his hand he would have been certain that he had dreamt the whole thing. He had never questioned what his gran had said or asked him to do. He had always trusted her and knew that what happened tonight was in some way a sign from her that she was still with them.

Later that evening when everyone had dispersed to various parts of the house, David went to thank his gran for the gift, but the blank stare was still there. No matter how hard he tried he just could not reach her so he gave her a kiss on the cheek and said good night.

David was sitting in his bedroom the next morning. It was a small square room with a tiny window that overlooked the lane at the front of the cottage. It had dark beams that ran the length of the room and a ceiling that sloped from the middle down towards the window. He was thinking back to the holidays he had spent in this cottage, many happy times, in this very room. He lifted the pendant that was hanging around his neck. The stone in the middle looked normal now, not at all how it had looked the previous evening.

David wondered whether Gran would ever be her old self again. Just then there was a shout and loud footsteps on the landing. His bedroom door burst open and a very angry looking Jessica stormed in.

"What have you done with it?" she raged at him.

"I don't know what you are talking about," David returned.

"Yes you do, the box of stones that I had in my room, they have gone!"

"Gran's box?" David asked. "You can't have lost them. You know how much they mean to her."

"I looked at them a couple of days ago. I am sure I put it back in the same place," said Jessica. "It was a secret hidey hole that Gran showed me years ago."

They both went back to Jessica's room, but sure enough the box and the stones were gone.

"Do you think that we should tell Mum about this?" Jessica asked.

"No", replied David. "She has got plenty to think about at the moment and they might well turn up in a day or two."

Although, even as he said the words, he was not so sure that they would.

A few days passed and there was still no sign of the box. Meanwhile David and Jessica were kept quite busy getting ready for their return to school after their move. There was a bus that Jessica had to catch at 7.45 in the morning as she had further to travel and another one at 8.15 for David.

When the next morning came, their mother had everything prepared; lunches packed and, in David's case, a new uniform clean and pressed. Jessica left without even saying goodbye. Since the disappearance of the box she had been distant and gloomy and David could not help but think that there was something else on her mind. Mrs Trent had told David that she wanted to walk him to the bus stop. He would rather have gone alone, but he knew that it would make her happy so he just smiled and said okay. As they left the cottage and walked down the lane the sun was out and it was a beautiful autumn morning. The leaves on the trees were changing colour, from green to reds, yellows and browns. Even the air felt different - fresher, cooler - somehow preparing you for the cold months ahead. The sun, although shining, seemed to have lost its strength. The light it gave seemed to bathe everything in an orange haze. It only took them a few moments to reach the end of the lane.

There were already about eight or nine children waiting at the bus stop just around the corner. Much to David's relief, when his mother noticed the other children, she stopped, gave him a kiss on the cheek and said that she hoped he would make some new friends today. David parted from his mother without even a backward glance; he was looking forward to meeting the other children. As he approached the group he was initially met with blank looks. David put on his best smile and walked up to a dark haired boy who he thought must be his own age. The boy was standing slightly apart from the other children and looked rather surprised when David greeted him and introduced himself.

The boy glanced at the others. They all seemed to have resumed their own conversations, so he turned back to David.

"Ryan Walsh," he muttered. "That's my name. I live with my mum on the estate on the other side of the village. So you're the new kid are you? Where do you live?"

"Just up the lane here," replied David. "Wheelwright Cottage. It belongs to my gran."

Ryan gave him a strange look but said nothing.

Just then the school bus came around the corner and ground to a halt in front of them. David noticed that Ryan pushed his way to the front of the queue and disappeared from sight without even saying goodbye. David waited patiently for everyone else to get on board, then climbed the steps onto the very crowded bus. As he made his way down the aisle, he started to think that he was not going to find a seat, but there half way down he came across a young dark haired girl sitting on her own. As David looked at her he could not help thinking that she had the brightest aura he had ever seen. It was yellow like a buttercup but even brighter as if a light was shining through it. David came back to his senses to find people were staring at him. He was still standing in the same place. He hadn't even noticed that the bus had started moving. After another glance at the girl, who did not even appear to have noticed him standing there, David sat down in the seat next to her. Then something strange happened. All the cacophony that David had become accustomed to hearing, when he was around other people (all their thoughts, all their future happiness), just seemed to fade away until he felt he was sitting all alone. It was so peaceful! David had not realised how loud and intrusive the voices and images had become. Sitting in this blissful silence felt like the sweetest rest he had had for a very long time.

All too soon the bus journey was over. Everyone streamed off the bus and headed for the main building. David found his way to the secretary's office. She was a large round woman, with curly black hair and a large round pair of glasses that made her look like one of those pop-eyed goldfish that seem to wiggle rather than swim. With his new timetable in his hand, David set out to find his classroom. It was not a large secondary school, but even so there seemed to be so many corridors leading all over the place. He stopped in the middle of a hallway and shut his eyes for a moment. When he opened them again, he set off purposely down the corridor to his left and came to a halt outside the third door on the right. He could hear a soft, gentle, woman's voice calling a register. David took a deep breath and opened the door.

"Hello there," said the teacher with the gentle voice. "You must be David Trent. Come in and find a seat. Look there is one over there next to Susan Gent."

David glanced around at the sea of faces and there, sitting by the window, was the girl from the bus. Once again she was sitting alone, although from the smile that was on her face you would never have guessed that she was obviously being avoided by the other children. David made his way across the classroom and even as he sat down on the seat next to Susan, the girl gave no sign that she had even noticed him. Just as before in the bus, David became aware of the restful silence descending. Sitting there next to this strange girl, he felt more relaxed with her than he had with anyone else for a very long time. David was delighted to find that he would be in all the same classes as Susan and that sitting with her meant that he would be able to concentrate on his studies without the constant distractions he had experienced in his previous school.

During the lunch break, David wandered around the playground talking to people and laughing at their jokes and banter. However he was reminded of his old school; so many children all willing to talk and share a joke but always a distance between them that he could not cross. Knowing people's private thoughts and dreams stopped you bonding with them. Although he could sense that they liked him and enjoyed his company, it was just not the same.

The school day ended and David found himself again sitting next to Susan on the bus. As the bus rumbled along he allowed his thoughts to wander. He found himself thinking about the missing box of jewels. The more he thought about it, the more it seemed that only one person could have taken them. He resolved to try and speak to Gran as soon as he could without attracting his family's attention. As he made to leave his seat he turned to say goodbye to the girl still sitting there. There was no response; not that he had really expected one but he felt the need to say it anyway.

David stepped down from the bus and started out for home. He hadn't even lived in the cottage for a week, yet it seemed so natural to be walking up the lane towards his new home. As he approached the cottage he could hear the sound of a high pitched engine and as he got closer he could see clouds of smoke billowing over the hedge. He pushed open the garden gate and found a short bearded man brandishing a chain saw walking across the lawn towards his father. David thought it looked like a scene out of a bad horror movie and might have been rather concerned for his father's safety if he had not seen that the man had a calm orange aura surrounding him. David knew that he could not be a mad murderer planning to kill his father.

David waved to the two men and carried on into the house where he found his mother was waiting for him in the kitchen.

"Have you had a good day, dear?" she asked. "Did you meet anyone nice?"

David reflected briefly about all that had happened and simply said, "Yes, it was fine Mum. It was just school you know."

Chapter 4

THE BROKEN SILENCE

The days passed.

Before long it was Friday afternoon and David was finally taking the last bus journey of the week. David had found out quite a bit about Susan Gent. She was not very popular at school because she made no attempt to talk or interact with anyone. According to another girl - Amy Skinner - in David's class, who had once been best friends with Susan when she was younger, Susan had never been quite the same since her mum and dad were killed in a car accident. Only Susan had survived. She now lived with her aunt, a very stern and strict woman called Miss Joan Harper. They also lived in Lower Hamdon, in a house called The Manse, at the smarter end of the village.

"Miss Joan Harper always looks like she has a bad smell under her nose," sighed Amy. "And when I called round after the accident to see Susan, she would not even let me through the front door, miserable old bat."

Susan was not the only person the other children talked

about. Ryan, the boy David had met at the bus stop, apparently was the school bully and most of the children avoided him. So far David had not encountered Ryan on a bad day. However, as he sat down next to Susan on the bus all that was about to change.

Ryan entered the bus just after David and had sat down in the seat opposite him. He sat staring at David as if waiting for everyone's attention. David glanced at him and noticed that his aura, which on their previous meeting had been bright green, now swirled with dark streaks in a very threatening way.

"I thought that there was something weird about you," Ryan growled accusingly at David. "You live with the old witch in the witch's house!"

"My gran is not a witch," David exclaimed. "She is a very kind woman, and she has helped many people including your mother."

David stopped as quickly as he had started. He should not have said that. Yet again he had not been able to stop himself saying exactly what he was feeling. He glanced at Ryan whose face had gone bright red and not in a good way.

"My mother would not go and see an old crackpot witch,"

Ryan blustered. "And if she isn't a witch why has she got those ugly looking monsters on her gate posts then?"

Before David could think of an answer, a voice from beside him calmly stated, "Actually those monsters are gargoyles and everybody knows that they are guardians against evil; that is why they have them on churches."

There was a deathly hush. David turned to look at Susan. Her face, normally so blank and expressionless, was now full of colour and life and she had fire in those green eyes which seemed to glow so brightly. It was only David who saw that her yellow aura was shining like the very sun itself. As David turned round, he was just in time to see Ryan storm off down the bus; his aura was now so dark it was hard to see the bright green it had once been.

"Don't mind him," said Susan. "He has problems of his own. You are David Trent, aren't you? My aunt mentioned that you had come to live with your gran. They used to be good friends you know. I do not know what happened but they don't even speak now."

David sat looking blankly at her. Up until now she had not spoken a word and all of a sudden she was telling him things about his own gran that he didn't know.

"Right this is your stop," Susan stated. "Have a good weekend and I will see you on Monday."

Totally amazed, David stepped down from the bus and stood watching it rumble away. It took him quite a few minutes before he was able to gather his thoughts and head home up the lane.

It was only as he was walking up the garden path that he remembered that he had wanted to ask Gran about the box of jewels. Why had he forgotten about it and why had it just popped back into his mind this very moment? As he walked through the front door he met his mother coming from the kitchen with a cup of tea in her hand. She gave David one of her sideways looks as he dumped his school bag on the hall table.

"I don't think that belongs there does it?" she said. Then in the next breath, "Oh my goodness!"

David followed his mother's gaze into the sitting room where his gran was sitting in her usual chair with Joe playing at her feet. It was only then he noticed that there on the floor in front of her chair was the small wooden box - the very same wooden box that had gone missing. It was lying wide open and precious stones were scattered all over the floor.

Mrs Trent rushed forward, trying not to spill the tea.

"He's far too young to be playing with those, Mother," she gasped. "He could have swallowed any of them!"

Gran simply sat in her chair as if oblivious to anything going on around her. Although David was sure that he had glimpsed her smile, and as he looked down at his younger brother, he wondered what was on her mind. As Mrs Trent had hurried to pick up all the stones off the floor, Joe had reached forward and taken hold of one of his mother's fingers. Just for a split second, there appeared a flash of light. To anyone else, it could have been merely the light from the window reflecting off David's mother's wedding ring, but to him it was like the glow of light he had witnessed the evening Gran had given him his pendant - or was it something he had simply imagined?

"Come on don't just stand there," said his mother. "Come and give me a hand. I still have the tea to put on and your father will be home soon."

David carefully picked up the rest of the stones, placed them back in the box, then followed his mother into the kitchen. He helped her peeling the vegetables and laying the table. Picking his moment, he asked her about Susan and her aunt.

"It's a very sad story you know," answered his mother. "Susan lost her parents a few years ago in a terrible car crash and that aunt of hers turned into a very bitter woman. She was not always like that though. When I was a child she was quite different. She used to visit us often and she was involved in all the village goings-on. Then, well, I don't know! There was some kind of disagreement between her and your gran. Something about a boyfriend she had had and they haven't spoken since. Although Mum did say to me later that she had no grudge with Joan; that it was all one-sided and that what she had told Joan had been for her own good. Anyway that's enough of all that, haven't you got some homework to do before we eat?"

David went out of the kitchen only to be met by Jessica coming through the front door.

"Follow me," said David. "I have got something to tell you."

They went up to David's bedroom and there he explained that somehow it had been their gran who had taken the box although they could not work out how. Without saying a word, Jessica lifted the front of her T-shirt just far enough to show David her belly button. David had known that she had had it pierced for her last birthday. When he looked a bit closer, he saw that it was set with a large ruby. He was sure it was one of the rubies that had once lived in the small wooden box.

"Gran gave this to me just before she went to London," explained Jessica. "Although I should really say she gave it back to me! She first gave me that ruby set in a ring for my last birthday, but when I became a goth, I stopped wearing it. She got quite upset and asked for it back. I was shocked at the time that she would take back a present but only a few days later she met me after school and gave it back to me, remade like this. She told me that I could wear it all the time and it would not clash with what I was wearing."

David felt inside his school shirt and lifted out his pendant.

"Why do you think she wants us to wear these gemstones?" he asked.

"I don't know," answered Jessica. "But it seemed really important to her and with what's happened to her now it just makes me feel closer to her."

"Has she said anything to you since she was brought back

from London?" queried David.

"No! Don't be silly David. She hasn't spoken to anyone. You know that!" retorted Jessica.

David said nothing. Surely she would not believe him if he told her. She would just think he was going mad. Why had Gran given them gemstones if they didn't possess gifts or have a knowledge of the family's history? Jessica left David sitting on his bed. He had never discussed his abilities with her - although many times he had wanted to, now being one of them. Well at least now he had someone to talk to. Or did he? Was this break in her usual silence just a momentary thing? Would Susan be back to her old distant aloof self again on Monday?

Chapter 5

THE UNWELCOME VISITOR

David mounted the bus with great trepidation when Monday morning came around. As he slipped into his usual seat, he thought for one moment that he had imagined it, that she had never spoken. Susan looked just the same pleasant but distant girl he had first met. Then, as if someone had turned on a light switch, she came to life.

"Did you have a good weekend then?" she asked. "I did. I got all my homework finished, so Aunt Joan let me go with her to town on Saturday and we had a lovely cream tea at a place overlooking the park."

As David looked at this strange girl, she seemed so different, so full of life - so happy it seemed. What had caused this transformation? He still experienced the same feeling when he was with her, the same quiet descended, but somehow it now seemed lighter, no longer so overpowering. Now that he had someone to talk to, he found that he spent most of his time in and out of classes with Susan. Even though she spoke quite freely when they were alone, she tended to clam up when other children were around and the content of their conversations was always very light. She never gave any suggestion of why she had been so distant at the start nor what had brought about the change.

That afternoon they were in an English class listening to Miss Brightman, who was also their form teacher, the lady with the soft voice that he had heard that first day waiting outside the classroom door. Miss Brightman was reading them the first chapter of the book she had set for homework. It had dawned on David that although Susan had let her guard down a little, he still couldn't sense what or how she was feeling. This had never happened to him before. Generally the more time he spent with someone the easier he usually found it to tune in. So as he glanced around to where Susan was sitting, he made a concerted effort to reach out with his mind. Not only was he met with a blank wall but she turned around and gave him a sharp look.

"That's very rude!" she exclaimed. "If you want to know what I am thinking you should just ask!"

David was so taken aback that he could feel himself going quite red. He looked away and did not dare look back for the rest of the lesson. When they left the classroom, Susan had rushed ahead and when he caught up with her she looked like she had been crying.

"I am so sorry," apologised David. "I did not mean to pry or upset you."

"I thought you were different," she countered. "My thoughts are my own and I don't wish to share them."

"I really am sorry and I promise that I will never try anything like that again," squirmed David.

There were so many things he wanted to ask her but he felt that now was not the right time. Susan gave him a little smile and moved off towards their next class.

"There is a fair coming to Braunton next week, had you heard?" she remarked some time later.

"Yes. Yes I had actually. I was going to ask my mum if we could go."

This was in fact a lie. He had not heard about it at all but he had seen it in the thoughts of others - even his mother had revealed it, without realising, that she had planned to take them all as a treat.

"Would you like to come with us or will you be going with your aunt?" David asked Susan.

"Well," responded Susan. "After the fair has finished at

Braunton it's coming to the village you know but only for one night. I was going to ask my aunt this evening if we could go."

I would think that the fair is not really her cup of tea, David thought to himself. He could not imagine anything that would be her cup of tea, other than sucking on a lemon. From what people had said about her, she sounded very cold and bitter - not the sort to enjoy herself at all.

He waved to Susan as the bus departed and turned for the short walk up the lane. As he reached the garden gate, he could see his mother sitting in the garden with a man whom he recognised as Fred Dingle the postman. Standing in the gateway David became aware of a strange warm feeling flooding his chest and then his vision was blurred. When it cleared again instead of looking at his new home, he was seeing Fred all dressed up in a suit, with a bunch of flowers in his hand approaching some steps up to a front door. As David kept watching, Fred made his way up the steps and pushed the door bell. However just as the door was opening, David's sight blurred again and he was back in the garden. Slightly shaken, he made his way up the path where he was met by his mother. Still in conversation with Fred, she did not notice that David looked a little pale. Fred said his goodbyes and ruffled David's hair as he passed him.

"That's the second visitor I have had today," said Mrs Trent. "The first one was a man called Major Reginald Steven. A friend of your gran's, so he said. Although she never mentioned that she knew him to me. When I was still living at home, we used to hear tales from the village about him. He was always travelling. They say his time in the army gave him the thirst for it. He was never at home. I don't think that I had ever met him before until today. The major had heard that your gran was not well so he kindly popped in to see how she is. He was very upset. Said that he owed her a lot and asked if there was anything he could do. Well of course I said no, but as we were talking I mentioned that I was looking for work and he told me that he was looking for someone to reorganise his library. Apparently it's in a shocking state. I told him that it was not really my area of expertise but that if I could find someone to help around the house I would give it a go. Anyway we can't stand here chatting. Change your clothes and you can help me get some vegetables from the garden."

David made his way up to his room. He was quite

overcome by what had happened so when a moment later the room started to darken he did not initially notice. Then there was a loud whining sound which seemed to go right through him. David glanced out of the window. How strange, he thought. The sun was shining just as brightly as it had been, but the light still seemed to be disappearing.

Just then there was a loud knock at the door and he heard his mother make her way from the kitchen to the front door. Sensing that something was not right, he left his bedroom and went to the top of the stairs but when he was just halfway down he stopped just as his mother opened the door. There in the doorway was what appeared to be a little old woman. When she spoke her voice seemed soft and alluring but David was not fooled. Her aura was as black as the night sky and there was still that awful whining sound coming from somewhere.

"Would you buy a bunch of heather?" said the old woman to Mrs Trent. "It will bring you good luck."

Mrs Trent, being the kind generous person that she was, reached inside her apron and produced her purse from which she handed the woman some money. David noticed that as his mother reached out her hand, the bracelet, set with large pieces of turquoise, that she always wore, slid down her arm and into view. The old woman retracted her hand so quickly that the change fell onto the floor. As Mrs Trent bent down to pick up the money, the old woman's eyes flew around the room and came to rest on David perched on the stairs. Her gaze was so piercing that he felt he could not look away. As his mother straightened up, he was sheltered from the old woman's gaze.

He heard her say, "Let Madam Serina read your palm my dear for being so kind to an old woman."

Mrs Trent, being too polite to dismiss the old woman, held out her right hand.

"Oh no my dear. The other one if you don't mind."

As the old woman reached out and took hold of his mother's hand, David instantly became aware of the large garnet ring on her finger. It seemed to suck the light from its surroundings - never becoming any brighter than a small black hole. The moment she grasped his mother's hand, the whining noise increased and was now joined by another unfamiliar sound.

It was Joe! He was crying - actually screaming. Joe rarely cried, certainly not like that. It was so shrill and unnatural.

Just as David's ears were becoming accustomed to it, the phone also began to ring. David looked down at his mother. Lost in the woman's whispering voice, she seemed totally unaware of any of the noises or strange things going on around her.

"Your poor mother. She is so ill, she is. But I see children - lovely sweet children. You have been blessed."

Although the voice sounded sweet and convincing, David noticed that the woman's face was set like a stone and as she held his mother's hand, he could see, much to his horror, that his mother's aura was fading as if being drained away. He felt frozen to the spot. He knew he should do something but what? And all the time the noise continued getting louder and louder by the moment.

"Travel I see on the horizon for you and a new job," the old woman crooned.

Then, as if from nowhere, a large ginger cat appeared on the doorstep. The old woman dropped Mrs Trent's hand as if she had been stabbed hard with a sharp stick, turned and disappeared across the garden. David ran to his mother's side.

As she came round from her trance-like state, she said,

"It's okay. I just came over all faint for a moment. Where did that nice old lady go?"

She did not seem to have realised what was going on and, to David's surprise, all the odd sounds had instantly stopped.

"I think I will just go and have a little lie down for a while - just to clear my head," said Mrs Trent.

As she turned away, David made his way out of the front door to look where the old woman had gone as she had not headed down the garden path. He was just in time to see her squeezing through the gap in the hedge which had been made by the fallen apple tree. Then she was gone. David stood there for what must have been almost five minutes. He then was startled by the sound of the telephone ringing. He ran back inside to pick up the telephone before it disturbed his mother. It was a very irate Jessica.

"What's been going on?" she demanded. "I have been trying to reach you. Why did no-one answer the phone?"

David, trying to sound as normal as possible, told her that their mother had been speaking to someone at the door and that he had been checking on Joe for her. He tried to reassure her that everything was fine. David was not sure that she sounded convinced, but she told him that she would be home as quickly as she could and rang off.

His head still whirring, David headed upstairs to check that his younger brother was alright. He walked into the nursery and looked into the playpen. Joe was fine. You would not have known that only minutes before he had been screaming his head off - and his gran was sitting peacefully, rocking gently in her chair. To stop himself from becoming lost in his thoughts David decided that he would head back into the garden and collect the vegetables his mother had mentioned and then make a start preparing the tea. Anything was easier than trying to make sense of it all.

Chapter 6

A NEW HELPER OR TWO

The next morning found David sitting on his bed still in the same confused state. He could not make sense of it at all - the vision; the strange woman; the weird noises or the appearance of the ginger cat. The only thing that he knew for certain was that he needed to talk to someone, so he stood up and made his way to Gran's room. She was wide awake, but even before he started to speak to her, he knew that he would not get a response. She looked at him and gave a little smile but that was it, no sign of any understanding at all. There was nothing else for it, he was going to have to talk to Susan. Goodness knows what she was going to say but after the previous encounter with her, he felt that she might not be quite as surprised as anyone else would be.

David finished dressing and made his way down for breakfast. He found his mother sitting in the kitchen. She looked a little pale but when David asked she said she felt a lot better. He put his empty cereal bowl in the sink, kissed his mother goodbye and made for the front door. Just as he reached the door, the bell rang. He stood mesmerised, and then with a shaking hand opened the front door. Much to his relief he was met by a young woman with a pale but smiling face.

"I have come about the job dear," stated the woman. "Is your mother in?"

David called for his mum, then passed the woman and headed off for the bus. Mrs Trent invited the woman in, thinking it funny as she was sure that she had not mentioned it to anyone but the major that she was looking for help and he had responded that he did not know of anyone.

"Millie Watson, that's my name," said the woman. "And I know that this is going to sound quite mad but I was visited by a fortuneteller last night who told me that I would find a job on the doorstep and gave me your address! Well I have been looking for a job in the village for ages and this seemed too good to be true so here I am."

Mrs Trent and Millie talked for some time about what the job entailed. Millie had looked after her own aged parents until they had passed away. She also had helped out at the local day care centre and was used to small children. So helper number one was hired.

"You're very distracted this morning," said Susan after David had failed to answer her for the third time.

"We need to talk."

"I thought that was what we were doing."

"Not here! We might be overheard."

Susan looked at him in a slightly concerned way. "When then?" she asked.

"Let's find a quiet corner at lunchtime," he replied.

Susan was now worried. She had never seen David like this. He was usually so bright and cheerful.

The morning dragged slowly by. David still had no idea of quite what he was going to say to Susan and what her reaction was going to be. Eventually they were huddled in a sheltered corner of the playground. The days were starting to become colder and as they were both pulling on their coats, David blurted out, "There is something really weird going on. I know I sound bonkers but just let me finish before you say anything."

Without looking at Susan, David recounted the previous day's happenings and did not stop until he had told her everything. Hesitatingly he then met her gaze expecting to see a look of horror on Susan's face, but instead she looked totally unfazed.

"I know," she said in a matter of fact way. "I am just glad that now I am not the only one that thinks so."

David stood there with his mouth open as if someone had just slapped him with a wet fish.

"Well most people round here might be as blind as bats," Susan exclaimed. "But that does not mean that I am."

"What? How? I mean when?"

David's brain just did not seem to want to be able to cope with any more surprises. Susan gave him a sympathetic pat on the arm.

"Strange things have been going on here well before you arrived. It did not take me long to realise that it all seemed to happen every year about the same time. Always when the fair was around. It started with people becoming ill. Then things and people go missing. Last year Mrs Miller disappeared. Her husband was told by the fortuneteller at the fair that she had run away with another man and that he should never go looking for her. From what I heard he never did but no- one else has heard from her either. There is so much more. Why don't you come home with me this afternoon? There is something you need to see."

For the first time in ages David was not able to concentrate on his studies and very nearly ended up in detention for not answering one of Miss Brightman's questions. During the afternoon break David went to the secretary's office and managed to phone his mother to ask her for permission to go to Susan's after school. Mrs Trent had assured him that she would speak with Aunt Joan and if it was okay with Joan she would get a message to him. Sure enough during double English a girl delivered a note to say that was fine and that his mum would pick David up later.

The bus journey had never gone so slowly, not helped by Susan refusing to tell him any more until they were home. She simply chatted away about everyday things which was driving David quite mad. Before long they were standing outside The Manse, Aunt Joan's house. How fitting it was - stark and unwelcoming. The garden was made up of small clipped bushes that looked as if they would not dare drop a leaf out of place. There was not a flower in sight. Susan seemed quite relaxed here and skipped up the front steps. Something about this place seemed familiar to him but David could not remember why.

Aunt Joan appeared in the hall as soon as they had shut

the door.

"Take your shoes off," she barked. "I do not want mud traipsed around my house."

David turned to face the woman with such a stern voice. She was tall - taller than most men in the village. Her features were hard and set and her dark hair was tied back in a tight bun but for all this there was a warmth to her aura that David found quite surprising. Today was just full of surprises.

"There is milk and biscuits in the kitchen. Mind you don't drop any crumbs."

They made their way into the kitchen and there on the table were two glasses of milk and a plate with four biscuits neatly arranged on it.

"She is not as bad as she seems," Susan whispered. "She has been very good to me and I love her dearly."

How confusing. David had never met anyone with such a conflicting aura. He would need to spend more time here to get a handle on it.

"She warned people, you know," stressed Susan. "Many times I heard that she had advised people not to go to the fair but most of them could not see the harm and afterwards they just seemed not to remember. When I first started to notice things, I could not make any sense of it so I started going to the library and researching it. They did not have many books on the subject and at first I did not even know what I was looking for and it was not until a month ago that I found it. When the library was not much help, I started looking in second-hand bookshops. One day I was rummaging through a box of slightly damaged books and there it was. Come with me. It's in my bedroom."

David made to run out of the room. He could not wait to see what she had found. Susan grabbed him by his arm. "Don't run. We don't want Aunt Joan to get upset and not let you come round again."

So slowly and quietly they made their way up the stairs and into Susan's bedroom. There she went to her dressing table and opened a large folder covered in flowery paper and produced what looked like a shabby old diary. On closer inspection it was a book with most of its cover damaged and ripped, but you could just about read the words that were printed on the cover.

"*The Search For Hope*," by Edna Sharp. David read the title several times. Surely there must be many Edna Sharps? His mother had never mentioned that Gran had written a book.

"What is it about?" asked David.

"Well. I have not finished reading it yet but it seems to be about a young woman who has certain abilities. She can hear the thoughts of others and can predict a little of the future. When she started writing the book her gifts were not very strong and she felt that she had no control over them. She wrote the book over a twenty year period. The point where I have got to in the book she has managed to contact other people with the same sort of gifts. On her travels she had discovered that in many cultures precious stones are used to help with healing and soothing. After much experimenting she had found the stone that worked best for her. The stone in itself has no power but helps the possessor to channel their thoughts. The young woman had started to enlist the help of others and one by one she had helped them to find the stone that would be right for them."

"Susan. David," called Aunt Joan. "David's mother has arrived to pick him up." David looked down at his watch. Had they really been talking for over an hour?

"We will have to continue this another time. Try and finish the book as soon as you can Susan."

Mrs Trent was waiting on the doorstep. David turned to

Aunt Joan and thanked her for allowing him to come over and as he did so he almost thought that he saw her features soften a little. David said next to nothing on the way home but his mother hardly noticed. She was so busy telling him about Millie and that she was going to start straight away.

When they reached the cottage, the first thing David noticed was that the large ginger cat was sitting by the gate post. It did not even move when he reached out to stroke it as he passed. It just started purring very loudly, then stood up and followed them up the path towards the house. As Mrs Trent opened the door it shot past her and ran up the stairs.

"Now where does he think he is going?" laughed Mrs Trent. "Could you find him for me and put him back outside?"

David made his way upstairs and searched all the bedrooms. At last he spotted a ginger tail poking out from behind Joe's playpen. As he got closer, he noticed that Joe was reaching through the bars and trying to poke the cat in the eye, but instead of getting cross it just kept rubbing its head on Joe's hand. The cat put up no fight as David picked him up but just continued to purr right up to the point that David shut the door behind it. David went through to the kitchen to give his mum a hand.

"If you peel the potatoes for me, I will get the washing off the line," his mother said.

He had almost finished by the time she returned. She put the washing basket on the table and started to prepare dinner. As David turned from the sink he saw that something was moving in the washing basket. As he moved closer, a ginger head suddenly appeared followed by a large body.

"Mum, look!" he exclaimed. "I think we have a stowaway."

Mrs Trent burst out laughing and before either of them could stop it the cat had jumped out of the basket and disappeared into the hall. David had a really good idea of where to look this time and sure enough there it was in Joe's room again. Four times the cat managed to get back in the house in the next half hour and each time it went straight to Joe's room. David's mother had him check that all the windows were shut and asked him to leave a note on the front door to tell everyone not to let the cat in. Even so when Mr Trent came home it managed to dash into the house in between his legs. Dad did not seem worried about it and said perhaps it should stay as he was convinced that he had heard mice in the attic. It took quite a bit of convincing but finally when the rest of the family had ganged up on her, Mrs Trent relented and said that the cat could stay but if the owner could be found, the cat would have to be returned to them.

So helper number two had arrived and David was convinced that its arrival was no coincidence. Only time would tell, but he felt he would sleep a little sounder knowing that the cat was in the house.

Chapter 7

A LITTLE BIT OF KNOWLEDGE

The next morning David woke up to the sound of rain against the window. He dressed and made his way down to the kitchen. As he walked through the door he was met by a mad mass of people and noise. Mrs Trent was starting her new job today, so as well as trying to get ready herself, she was telling Millie, who had come in early, what needed to be done. Jessica was storming round the room scowling at everyone. Her moods definitely seemed to be getting worse - especially since she had heard the fair was coming to Braunton. Joe, affected by the tension in the air, was busy trying to throw his breakfast across the room - most of which seemed to have landed on the cat who sat quite undisturbed at the side of his chair. Even Millie, who never seemed to get in a flap, was turning a little red in the face. David grabbed a piece of toast and decided it would be easier to keep well out of the way especially as he had so much to think about. He sat down in the window seat in the sitting room, so deep in thought that he hardly noticed the rain had been joined by a strong howling wind.

"Come on," shouted his mother. "You are going to miss the bus if you don't run."

David glanced down at his watch. Had he really been sitting there for forty minutes? He grabbed his coat from the rack in the hall, pulling it on as he ran down the lane. He was only just in time as the last person was climbing the steps of the bus. Still panting, he collapsed into the seat next to Susan. She turned and looked at him with a little knowing smile.

"Gargoyles," she whispered and raised her eyebrows. He looked at her with a totally nonplussed expression. There was a silent pause.

"So?" David queried when he could not bear the silence any longer. Susan looked exasperated.

"That noise you heard the other day, when the old woman came to the house - the wailing noise - it was the gargoyles by the gate."

David sat up with a surprised start. "How do you know that?"

Susan went on to explain that it was all there in his gran's book. "Gargoyles are to ward off evil. They wail when they sense danger. The only reason that it didn't work was because the woman didn't enter through the garden gate but through the gap in the hedge - the gap left by the fallen apple tree. Even the hedge itself which runs all the way around the garden is a protective barrier. A ring of beech is said to be a good defence, but with the ring broken a weakness was found."

"I have so much more to tell you," said Susan as the bus pulled up outside the school. "I will tell you everything I know, but you must promise me one thing. I know this seems petty but you must assure me that you won't let this get in the way of your studies or mine."

David felt rather deflated, because he wanted to know everything now, but he knew that Susan would not be swayed in this so he agreed and they set off for their form room. Having made the decision, David found that he could quite easily focus on the lessons in hand and before he knew it, it was lunch time. He and Susan had taken to spending their lunch hours in the library so that they would not be disturbed. Susan started by saying that she was having trouble reading the book because there were parts of it written in foreign languages but that there was mention of the Circle of Hope - a group of people who wished to use their gifts to help people. However there had been one member - a man - who wanted to use the power of his gift for his own personal gain. Over a period of time he had become very rich and had started recruiting others and as time passed he even managed to reverse the ageing process so that he could stay looking young. However he could only do this by draining the life force of other people. The book did not go into detail about how this could be achieved, but David felt that what he had witnessed the day the fortuneteller had come to the house was just that. The book revealed that he had started to hunt down other members of the circle. Then when he destroyed their gemstones, they lost their gifts and became trapped in their own bodies.

David gasped. "Of course!"

That explained his gran's condition. According to Susan there was no mention of a cure; just that when someone used their gift to infuse an individual stone with energy, a strong bond was formed and it could not be undone.

David tried his best to focus throughout the afternoon, but all he could think about was reaching home to see his gran. He felt sure that her special gemstone must be the pink quartz set in the ring she always wore. Even when the school bell rang and he had run all the way to the school bus, it was another thirty minutes before he was able to jump off the bus and run up the lane towards the cottage. He paused momentarily on the doorstep to catch his breath. Then he reached out and with sweaty hands turned the door handle. As he walked into the kitchen he was not sure that he knew what he wanted to find out. If Gran's ring was undamaged then she was simply and sadly very ill, but if the ring was split in two it showed that she had been attacked by a power stronger than her own.

The back door was open and David caught sight of his mother in the garden collecting the washing from the line. His gran was sitting in her usual chair by the fire. She was staring into space. He took a deep breath and reached for her hand. Gently he turned her hand over and gasped. How had he not noticed it before? There was a clear crack nearly all the way through the stone. His head swam as he slumped down onto the floor next to his gran's chair.

Then as if in a dream he heard Gran's voice. "Come now, there is so much I must tell you. Pull yourself together! I don't have much strength left. Listen. Now that this travelling menace has shown her true colours something can and must be done. I know you found my book with a little help from your friend, but to read it you will need a code book to help you decipher it. You must visit the antique shop on the High Street in Braunton. Remember that I love you and will be watching over you for as long as I can." Her voice faded.

David's mind cleared instantly as if someone had thrown water in his face. He spun round, desperately wanting to see his gran's face smiling down at him, but before she came into focus, he knew that nothing had changed and that what he had heard had come from inside his own head. There was no doubt in his mind though that it was fact and that he must follow and carry out her instructions.

"Are you alright?" asked Mrs Trent as she came in from the garden. David looked up and tried to give her what he thought would be a cheery smile but, by the look on her face, he could tell that she was not convinced.

"Did you realise that Gran's ring was damaged?"

"Yes," she answered. "It must have been when she had her accident in London. I was going to take it to the jewellers but she got so upset when I tried to take it from her that I thought it best left. Now if you have some homework, please go upstairs and get it done before dinner."

David was halfway up the stairs before he realised that he had not asked his mother how her first day at work had been, but in his mind he glimpsed her smiling and laughing with Major Steven surrounded by piles of books and photographs and he knew it had gone well.

So he entered his bedroom with a slightly lighter heart.

Chapter 8

A STRESSFUL DAY

David had slept very little. Strange dreams had haunted him, and he was already up and dressed by the time his alarm clock started to clang its morning chorus. It would be Saturday before he would be able to go to Braunton and, as today was only Thursday, Saturday seemed a long way away. He had considered trying to persuade Susan to bunk off school for the day but as he knew she would never agree to it, he decided not to ask. As he ate his breakfast alone, he made a promise to himself that he would do everything in his power to find whoever was responsible for harming his gran and that he would follow her wishes and stop this evil menace.

Not being in the mood to talk to anyone, he left the house early and dawdled his way down the lane. He was the first person at the bus stop, though only by a few moments. As the other children slowly arrived he felt their overpowering thoughts and realised how much he had come to rely on Susan and the calming effect she had on his state of mind.

He made a mental note to ask her about it as soon as he saw her. However, yet again, things seemed to be conspiring against him. Susan was not on the bus.

By the time the bus reached the school gates, David had a pounding headache and, although the images from the other children were all happy ones, he was not sure he could face his first lesson. He decided to head to the first aid room to see if he could persuade the nurse to let him go home or at least sit the first period out.

The nurse, Miss Packman, was not known for her sympathetic nature, but David's luck was obviously changing for the better. She did not seem at all surprised to see him and when he explained how he felt, she said soothingly, "There there my dear. There is a lot of it going around at the moment. How about you lie down for a while and if you do not feel better, I will phone your mother to pick you up."

David was relieved to be able to rest in a quiet place with only one person's thoughts intruding on his. Miss Packman, it seemed, was planning a well earned holiday to Venice and visions of such a beautiful place helped to soothe his mind.

He was not sure how long he had been lying there but the sound of someone knocking at the door brought him back to his senses. Even before the door had opened he could feel it was Susan. His mind had already started to clear and he could even see her bright yellow aura shining from under the door.

"I feel so much better," he found himself saying to Miss Packman.

"Well if you are sure my dear," she answered.

Before the door had closed, David started telling Susan about the previous night's events. He hardly drew breath until he had told her the whole story. Then before Susan could respond in any way, he launched into questioning her about her ability to shield her thoughts.

By the time he had finished, David was red in the face and quite out of breath. As he glanced across at Susan, he was shocked to see her looking quite stern. Finally as she seemed to gather her thoughts, her features softened and she began by addressing David's issue with her being able to shield her thoughts.

David knew that Susan's parents had been killed in a car crash. It seemed to many people that Susan had adjusted quite well to this tragedy. However, the story she recounted to David of the weeks after the accident was of a person who had shut herself off from the outside world. With only her ice-cold aunt for company, Susan had retreated into herself as a way of masking the pain. It was not until months later she began to realise that the mental strength she had developed allowed her to cope with everyday life. So on the day she sensed David trying to invade her mind she had - without thinking - blocked him. Only later had she realised what she had done and the implications. After Susan had finished speaking, they both sat in silence feeling rather overwhelmed.

Susan was the first one to speak.

"Oh fudge!"

She had glanced at her watch. Break time had finished five minutes ago and they were going to be late for their double history lesson. Luckily Mr Campbell considered them both to be model students so he made very little fuss. When the end of the day finally came, it was difficult for them to carry on their conversation with so many other people around. Susan always carried her mobile phone with her so they decided to see if David's mother would agree to pick him up from Susan's again later. Mrs Trent said that it would be okay for him to go to Susan's house and she would ask his father to pick him up on his way home from work at six o'clock.

At last they exited the bus outside The Manse. Aunt Joan would not be home until five thirty so they had an hour of freedom in which to converse without being interrupted. Susan stated she was glad that there was someone else to help with the translation of the book. She had been struggling and was convinced that some of the text was not even in a modern language.

"Well the only way we are going to find out is by going to the antique shop and asking, isn't it?" questioned David.

Susan was not sure this was a good idea but, as she could not come up with an alternative plan, she conceded it was the only way to go. Saturday morning was the obvious choice. Aunt Joan always helped out at the library so transport there would not be a problem and as David had all his homework completed up-to-date, he knew his mother would not object to him accompanying Susan.

David had been waiting for the right time to ask and now seemed to be as good as any. "Susan," he began cautiously. "Now don't get angry or anything, but I wondered if you might consider letting your guard down long enough for me to see your thoughts. It might give us some insight into whether we might find what we are looking for."

Susan gave a little smile.

"I wondered how long it would be before you asked me that. I have been giving it some thought and I am as curious as you to see not only the future but whether I can control it enough for that. I have never tried to let my guard down before. I just hope I can get it back up again as I am not sure I could cope without it."

"I promise you I will stop any time you want me to," David reassured her.

They sat in the middle of the sitting room floor facing each other. Slowly David reached out with his mind. At first he found the same impenetrable wall he had encountered before, but gradually it softened until it melted away and images started to appear. At first they were hazy but as his vision cleared David could see Susan. She looked so pretty. Her hair had been arranged in curls and she was wearing a long pink dress. Familiar music played in the background and beautifully coloured stained glass windows glowed all around her. Then he saw Susan scattering rose petals on the ground and heard bells ringing. He glimpsed a sea of faces. Suddenly the music changed. David felt as if time had moved on. It was now evening and there was a party in full swing. Scouring the room he finally located Susan just outside a pair of French doors. At first he thought she was alone but then an arm appeared around her waist. David strained to see more clearly. As she turned, the face of a dark-haired boy came into focus and, as David watched, the boy bent forward and kissed her. As the youth looked up, David could have sworn that when their gazes met the boy winked at him.

The shock made him tear his mind away. He jumped to his feet and turned away from Susan so as not to let her see that he had gone red. David was not sure why he felt so affected by Susan kissing a strange boy but he could not shake the feeling. When he regained his composure he turned and was shocked to see Susan still sitting on the floor with her eyes closed. He spoke her name loudly but she did not respond. He walked quietly towards her and placed his hand on her shoulder. At his touch she stirred and her eyes slowly opened. She looked tired and slightly sad.

"Are you okay?" David asked gently.

"I will be," she answered. "It took a lot of energy to rebuild something that had seemed so easy to let down."

Just then the door opened and Aunt Joan came in. As

soon as she saw them she started a long monologue about how bad her day had been and how incompetent other people were. Even when she finally walked through to the kitchen, she did not stop talking and complaining. This gave them just enough cover for David to describe to Susan what he had seen. A wedding was the most likely explanation but whose and when was not clear. David omitted the part about the dark-haired boy. He convinced himself it was not relevant.

"Well, we are not any further forward, are we?" queried Susan. "But one thing is for sure, it will be a long while before I try that again."

Noticing his worried look, Susan assured David that it was nothing he had done. Pushing her own mind herself had worn her out.

Mr Trent arrived just after six o'clock. This had enabled them to find enough time to discuss a plan for their visit to Braunton on Saturday. It all still seemed a bit vague and rather daunting but as David joined his father in their car, thoughts of his family sitting down to enjoy a family dinner slipped gently from his father's mind and David's mood instantly improved.

Chapter 9

GOOD DAY, BAD DAY

Friday passed uneventfully. David and Susan spent all their free time double checking all their homework was up to date, so that there would not be anything to prevent them from going to Braunton on Saturday morning. Susan reminded David that afternoon that there was only one more week before the fair arrived in Lower Hamdon. Time was running out.

Little time was left and so far they had found out next to nothing. David desperately hoped that tomorrow's trip would be more fruitful. So many times in the last few weeks, he had been tempted to speak to his mother about what was going on. However he was aware that it might raise too many questions - questions for which he did not have any ready answers, at least not yet and possibly never.

He stopped as he reached the garden gate and looked up at the cottage. It seemed so peaceful, yet moving here seemed to have been the catalyst for everything that was going on. Taking a deep breath he walked purposefully up the path and into the house. If he completed the history report he had been given today, he would be free of school work for the time being.

That evening at supper David was quite content to listen to his parents talking about their day and how their work was progressing. This normality was somehow reassuring. Mrs Trent was saying that her job with Major Steven was turning out to be far more interesting than she could have imagined. The major had travelled extensively and led such an interesting life. Mr Trent, on the other hand, was saying that he had decided that he would like to spend more time at home as Joe was growing up so fast and, with him being away at work all day, he hardly had a chance to see his youngest child. Mr Trent went on to say that he was looking into starting up a website from which to sell his craft material. It would mean employing someone to manage the shop, but as business was doing well it seemed quite a reasonable step to take.

It was only when David glanced around the table that he realised something was wrong. Jessica was always quiet at meal times these days but there was more to it than that. She looked so pale and her eyes seemed agonised. Even her aura, usually a deep claret red, was greatly diminished and lacking its usual vibrancy.

David came back to reality with a jolt. He was suddenly convinced that his sister's moods were somehow connected to what was going on. But in what way and how could he find out? So it was with a troubled mind he went to bed. He fell quickly into a restless sleep. A sleep where he saw people with no faces, chasing him - all demanding to know something. Yet he did not know what.

The next morning dawned grey and drizzly. Pushing all other thoughts aside, David felt positive that today would be the day he and Susan would discover information which would show them the way. Mrs Trent had already agreed to the trip, although David felt sure if she knew what was happening she would not have been so happy to give him permission.

It was a good fifteen minute walk to Susan's house. As he made his way through the village, people were going about their Saturday business. He was greeted by many as he walked and it made him realise why his gran liked living here and thought so highly of the local people. They were so welcoming - even though he didn't know many of them.

As he arrived outside their house, Susan and her aunt were just coming out of the front door. Susan gave him her little smile and Aunt Joan managed a rather stiff good morning. David wondered if her face would actually crack if she tried to smile. Everything about her gave the impression that she was covered in prickles. Maybe, he thought, she had been a hedgehog in a former life. David secretly shared this thought with Susan as they climbed into the back seat of the car.

The involuntary snort of laughter Susan gave prompted Aunt Joan to complain. "I hope you are not coming down with something. There are so many people ill at the moment. We will be so short staffed at the library that I expect I shall be left to do it all."

Susan assured her that she had just reacted to some dust and, really, she felt fine.

Braunton consisted of one long main street. During the summer it would be overrun with holidaymakers (or "grockles" as the locals liked to call them). However on a grey Saturday in October there were few people about. Half the shops were closed - there was not much call for kiss-me-quick hats, ice cream or suntan lotion in the middle of winter.

The library and main car park were situated at the far end

of the town. Here they parted from Aunt Joan and started what they hoped would be a successful quest for essential knowledge. Susan thought there were two antique shops. However they had no way of knowing which one they needed so they decided they would visit each one in turn and ask some discreet questions and see who produced the right answers.

The first one they came to was closed and judging by the content of the shop window it was more of a junk shop than an antique one. Trying to sound positive David suggested they should carry on. The second shop was round the next corner. It was exactly as David had imagined it would be. *"Smale's Antique Emporium"* the sign read and it looked like it had been there forever. The windows were so grimy it was almost impossible to see inside.

After loitering on the pavement for a short while, David hesitantly stepped forward and opened the door. There was a complaining groan, followed by a loud ringing from the bell hung just inside the door and activated by it being opened. As Susan and David made their way through the shop, the light grew dimmer and dimmer and the atmosphere became even gloomier. There were rows upon rows full of large dark pieces of furniture. They looked like they had come out of some medieval manor house or castle. None would have fitted into the majority of modern homes.

Finally they reached a glass-fronted counter at the back of the shop. Still no-one had appeared. They had just bent down to look inside a cabinet when there was a loud cough and there before them stood a young man in a bright pink T-shirt and ripped jeans. David could not help thinking that his hair looked like something that had escaped from a pet shop and on closer inspection he also saw that the young man had a ring through his nose. Both David and Susan were so taken aback by the man's appearance that even when he asked if he could help them all they could do was stand there with their mouths open.

"Listen - I can't stand around here all day," the young man snapped. "Are you lost or something?"

Politely David said the first thing that came into his head.

"Could we see the owner please? I believe he has something for me."

The young man widened his eyes as if he thought they were a bit simple. "I am the owner and I am sure I have nothing that would interest you."

It took David a few moments to gather his thoughts. When he and Susan had imagined meeting the proprietor of the antique shop, they had visualised someone elderly with grey hair and small round glasses.

David rallied and said, "I believe my grandmother left something with you for safe keeping. It's just that I need it now."

On hearing this the young man's face changed completely. He looked worried and shaken.

"I can't help you. Now if you don't mind I have work to do," he half shouted.

With this Susan's nerve failed and she retreated rapidly in the direction of the door. David, however, did not move and it was only when Susan had nearly reached the door that the man spoke again. His voice had softened and he was looking at David in a totally fascinated way.

"So you are David. I must admit I thought it would be a few more years before you came looking. If you had allowed me to see you straightaway instead of cloaking yourself it would have made this much easier from the beginning."

The young man, whose name turned out to be Frank, registered the puzzled expression on David's face because he then forthrightly explained that the gift he himself possessed was quite limited.

"It only allows me to read little things about people. Your gift must be very powerful to be able to shield yourself like that and your friend as well at the same time."

David turned and smiled at Susan, who had plucked up the courage to return, and said gruffly: "Well, we all have our secrets don't we? Now about this book?"

"Oh, yes," sighed Frank as he led them into the back room. They found themselves in a dark study full of books and many pictures of cats. There were cobwebs everywhere. Items furthest away looked like they had not been touched for some time. Frank went on to explain that he had inherited the shop when his father - who had been a great friend of Edna Sharp - had died. "Your gran is a very kind lady. She helped me develop my gift and entrusted the book to me for safe keeping." He noticed Susan glancing at all the cat pictures.

"Guardians you know about - as so many people do including my father when he was alive. Cats have been worshipped in many ancient cultures. They were said to guard your soul. It has been written that cats have the power to drink your breath and steal your life force while you sleep. Father believed they could sense evil and were compelled to protect the innocent. However I feel that you know this already."

"What do you mean?" gasped David.

"The evil!" he exclaimed. "It's all around. It seems to be sucking the life out of this town. I thought I might go and see the fortuneteller who travels with the fair. People say she is very good."

"NO!" shouted Susan and David simultaneously.

"She is somehow involved with all this. Her 'gift' is not used to help people," David added firmly.

It was nearly two hours later when they left the shop. They walked in silence, David carrying the small package they had been given by Frank. There was so much to think about. Susan eventually was the first to speak. She suggested that they should go to a small café near the library and have some lunch. Aunt Joan would be finishing her work in about half an hour and she would want to go straight home.

Luckily there were only a few people in the café so it was quite easy to talk without being overheard. They had decided before they had set out that they would not open the book in the antique shop. They agreed that although David's gran had entrusted the book to Frank, it was not clear how much Frank had been told.

Susan opened the small bundle containing the book. Like the other, it was small and diary-like. As she scanned through the pages, Susan could see there were many codes and languages listed from Latin to Sumerian. It seemed to both of them that it was going to take a lot more than six days to decipher even a quarter of it.

After a hurried lunch, they stood waiting for their ride home feeling mentally drained, exhausted and overwhelmed.

Susan said, "Well at least that explains why that old woman disappeared so quickly when Mungo (as the ginger cat was now called) arrived."

David nodded. He was glad there was something looking out for his family, but somehow he doubted that it would be enough protection from what lay ahead.

As David lay in bed that night his head was still spinning. He hoped that Susan was coping better. She seemed to have taken it upon herself to be in charge of deciphering the book. They had not really discussed it but there was an unspoken understanding that, as she clearly had more aptitude for this sort of task, the responsibility had fallen to her. David decided that he must try and talk to his gran again. Tomorrow seemed to be the most likely time as most of the family would be going to church and Millie would be busy with her chores.

The next morning, David woke with just one thing on his mind. It was some time before he managed to be alone with his gran. He found it took a lot more effort to reach her this time. Previously he simply had had to focus on her. This time he was sweating in frustration and starting to panic before he heard her voice.

The eventual response he received was not the soft greeting he had expected but a harsh tone as she scolded him for wasting his energy.

"My dear grandson - you will need all your strength if you are going to face her effectively. She is very powerful. The only information I can provide you is in the book. You must study it well." Then her voice softened. "I am so heartened that you have chosen to embrace your gift. Not everyone is strong enough to do so. Now listen - you must not attempt to communicate with me again. Not unless it is a case of life or death. It's not just your energy you are draining, it is mine too." With that, her voice trailed away and David was left with many unanswered questions.

As he returned to his own mind, he became aware of how exhausted he was. As David struggled to stand he caught sight of his gran's ring. He could see that the crack in the rose quartz gemstone was now nearly all the way through. Had this been progressively becoming worse or was it as a result of their conversation? With this thought David was flooded by a wave of guilt and he wondered if he would ever be able to speak to his gran again.

Millie, banging the back door shut, brought him to his senses. He quickly left the kitchen to prevent the housekeeper's thoughts invading his mind. He needed peace and quiet so sought the sanctuary of his bedroom. The last thing to enter his mind as he drifted off to sleep was the hope that Susan was making headway with the book.

David was woken by the sound of raised voices. Forcing himself alert, he made his way downstairs and paused outside the kitchen door which was slightly ajar. The voices he heard were that of Jessica and their father. This seemed wrong. They never usually argued. Jessica was Daddy's little girl.

As he listened, David could hear his sister's voice. "I can't stay. I have to go. Sarah's mum is picking me up in fifteen minutes."

A very exasperated Mr Trent pleaded, "Just tell us what's wrong. We can't help you if you won't tell us."

"It's nothing. I just need some peace and quiet to get my coursework done," Jessica replied firmly.

Even from outside the door David could tell she was lying. He could not bear it any longer. He pushed the door open and walked in as casually as he could. Silence fell over the room and everyone turned to look at him. As he caught his sister's eye, her tears, as well as her aura, gave away how upset she was. At the same time he experienced a vision - she was with her friends and she seemed a lot calmer and more relaxed. In that moment he knew he must convince his parents to let her go.

"What's all the upset?" he asked with as normal a tone as possible. "She just wants some peace and quiet. What's the problem with that? See you when you get back Jessica."

With that David turned and walked out of the kitchen. He continued down the hall and into the sitting room. There he found his gran sitting by the fire. As he walked over to her, he could see she was silently crying. He pulled a tissue out of the box on the coffee table and dried her tears.

"Don't worry Gran. As soon as I have dealt with Madam Serina, I promise I will find out what is wrong with Jessica. Maybe it is best if she is out of the way for now." He hoped rather than believed this to be true.

Shortly afterwards Jessica left. Her parents were so upset.

"I don't understand why she has to go for a whole week," Mr Trent said sadly. "She has been so down recently. I know she is at that difficult age, but I do worry about her."

David decided that he would go to bed early - hopefully tomorrow would be a better day.

Chapter 10

THE LONGEST DAY

David lay half awake, waiting for his alarm clock to go off. His sleep had been restless again. Like his parents, his concern for Jessica was nagging at the back of his mind - however much he tried to focus on the day ahead. Finally the small round clock clanged its morning chorus. As he dressed he could hear his parents moving around downstairs and guessed that they too had suffered a disturbed night's sleep. When he entered the kitchen, his parents' conversation came to an abrupt halt and they greeted him with what he guessed was meant to be a cheerful smile. The silence was so loud it was like someone screaming. Little did David realise that he would crave this silence before the day had ended.

Leaving the house early to escape the sombre and unsettled atmosphere, David wandered slowly down the lane. Standing at the bus stop with everyone else would mean starting his day with a severe headache, so he waited at the end of the lane until he saw the bus approaching. Walking slowly he timed it so he would be last on the bus and could be seated beside Susan in just a few moments and thereby shielded from the onslaught of the thoughts and excitement of all the others. Much to David's horror Susan was not on the bus and therefore any hope of escaping the tidal wave of emotions was gone.

The visions were so intense during the journey to school that David found he could not separate one from another. The only thing which made this bearable was the overwhelming delight of so many young people that the fair had arrived and would be opening to the public at the end of the week.

Instead of turning left once off the bus, David turned right and managed to hide behind the bus shelter until everyone else had made their way to their destinations. He then made his way to the nurse's room hoping for a repeat respite. He had contemplated asking another pupil if they knew why Susan was not at school but, as no-one else was particularly friendly with her, it seemed rather pointless. David paused outside the door of the nurse's room, then knocked and entered. As Miss Packman had been so sympathetic last time, he felt he could count on at least a few hours lying down somewhere quiet. But it was not meant to be. The face that greeted him was not that of Miss Packman but of a tall stone-faced woman. Her reaction was as negative as her looks.

"You look fine to me!" she snapped. "Go back to your class and stop bothering me. If Miss Packman had not gone and fallen ill I could be at home watching *Neighbours* and *Home and Away*."

Realising that there was no point in arguing with this harridan, David departed. Trying to do the right thing he headed off to first period history. He sneaked into the back of the class just in time to be handed a test sheet. Trying to ignore bombarding thoughts, he focused on the person in front of him - Stephen Brown. This turned out to be a blessing in disguise. Stephen was a smart kid who was really into history and every time he read one of the questions and knew the answer, the same one appeared in David's mind. By just homing in on Stephen the test and rest of the lesson went by quite quickly. However as he left the classroom David knew that his luck could not hold - so he made a run for it. Luckily no-one saw him leaving the school building. It was going to be a long day with nothing to do, especially without Susan to shield him. Going anywhere with anyone else was out of the question. A day alone wandering the fields behind the school was the only option and all he could think about was Susan and the book.

Finally the school day was over. Although he wanted to avoid the crowd he did not dare to miss the bus as that was the quickest and easiest way to travel to Susan's house. By the time he was climbing the steps to the old manse his head was spinning but before he could ring the bell, Susan had opened the door.

"I am so sorry about today," Susan apologised, looking concerned. "Aunt Joan has been so unwell I just couldn't leave her."

David smiled weakly and followed her into the kitchen where the book lay open on the table.

"Are you mad?" gasped David. "Leaving this where your aunt might see it!"

"She has not been able to get out of bed, let alone make it downstairs", retorted Susan with a stern look on her face. "Do you want to know what I have found out or not?"

David sat down a little sheepishly.

"Well, don't get too excited", she carried on. "Little of what I have managed to decipher has to do with Madam

Serina or how to get rid of her."

David tried to sit patiently as Susan told him about the information she had discovered - most of which was about the Circle of Hope and how it started. There was a list of the names of members but no contact details. Some were from this country, others from abroad. No dates had been included so some of the members might no longer be alive.

Susan explained that she had read about a ritual for how to bond with a gemstone and an explanation about how the strength of different gemstones depended on the strength of a person's gift. Gifts tended to fall into four categories - fortunetellers, healers, energy controllers and animal whisperers. Within these categories there were also many variations -from people who could sense a change in the weather to others who were able to influence people's thoughts and decisions.

By the time David had to leave, with all the information swimming around in his head, he felt that he was still no further forward. With her aunt being so unwell, Susan would not be at school tomorrow either. David started planning to fake an illness in order to ensure a day off school for himself too. He assumed that it would not be too difficult to do.

There had been so many people falling ill since the fair had arrived in town that no-one would be surprised if he had picked something up. There was one small snag however, his mother's keen sense for the truth.

David was heading out of the village when who should he see coming the other way but Ryan Walsh and judging by Ryan's raging aura he was out to cause trouble. David quickly decided the best policy was to keep his head down and pretend that he hadn't noticed Ryan. David held his breath as they drew level with each other expecting an onslaught of verbal abuse from Ryan but Ryan kept walking past. Just when David thought it was safe to relax, he was overwhelmed by the vision of a man lying in a hospital bed. The nurse standing by his bedside was assuring her patient that as he was now fully recovered, he was going to be discharged by the doctor and would be able to return home to his family tomorrow.

Realising the importance of what he had been shown, and without contemplating the consequences, he turned and ran after Ryan. Ryan spun round as David caught him by the shoulder. He was shocked to see the boy was crying.

"What the hell do you want?" Ryan spat.

David, not knowing the best way to tell him, blurted out: "It's okay. He'll be home soon. Your dad that is."

For a fleeting second there was a look of shock on Ryan's face. Then it changed into a mask of pure rage. "You think it's funny do you? My dad, a soldier, has been missing presumed dead while on a posting abroad." He faltered and seemed to shrink in size.

"No! Please believe me", David begged. "I can't explain how I know, but I really do. He is alright and he will be home with you tomorrow."

Ryan's expression turned from despair to uncertainty. "You're a witch aren't you?" he accused David. "Like that gran of yours! Why would you tell me such things if not to try and get back at me to punish me?"

"I'm no witch and nor is my gran. We just know things. That's all. We are allowed to visualise situations sometimes and sense other people's true feelings and emotions. I saw your father. He is in a hospital somewhere, but he is okay and he will be on his way home tomorrow."

Ryan seemed to regain his composure and his voice became threatening again. "If I find you have been winding me up, I swear I will punch your head off", he snarled and with that he stormed off.

Not knowing if he had done the right thing, David headed home. He found his mother and father in the kitchen. As he walked in, they once again stopped talking. He had taken this, over the last few days, to mean that they were discussing Jessica. Although she phoned every day, they were still convinced that she was hiding something and this made them puzzled and unhappy. Like his parents, David thought of his sister constantly and tried to comprehend the situation she had so firmly chosen. Since she had left home, he had only seen her once. Appearing happier than she had been for a long time, she was laughing and joking with a group of friends at the local shopping centre.

David launched straight into his dying swan act, claiming he felt weak and dizzy. When he announced he was going straight to bed without any supper, his father was convinced and started to fuss. But his mother seemed unmoved and simply stated that it was a good idea and that they would see how he was in the morning. Feeling disappointed that he had not yet achieved his goal, David brooded on what else he could do. If his mother could not be convinced, school for him tomorrow without Susan was not an option.

Chapter 11

A VISION OF WHAT?

All of a sudden he was running but from what he did not know. He was aware that Susan was by his side even though he could not see her. His legs could go no faster. Trying to focus on his surroundings was difficult. He was limited to seeing a few metres around him. Under his feet was long grass. Maybe he was in a field or pasture? Suddenly the light faded and the path narrowed. The air became cooler and stiller. Unexpectedly he and Susan found themselves changing direction away from the path and into the rough undergrowth. After ten metres, they were standing in front of a large oak tree. As they circled the trunk they discovered an old rope ladder with wooden rungs hanging from the tree. David encouraged Susan to climb first so that he could help her but as she placed her foot on the third rung it snapped. If David had not been close behind her she would have fallen to the ground. Somehow they managed to bypass the broken rung and proceed gingerly one rung at a time until they reached the top of the rope ladder where they found a trap door. As David followed Susan through it, a sudden sense of relief flooded his mind and he awoke with a start.

He sat up in bed. His hands were sweaty and he still felt a little out of breath. What he had experienced was very disturbing. Although he knew that the outcome of the vision was good, the fact that these images involved him gave him an uneasy feeling. Gran had always said that his gifts would grow and change, but she had never indicated in which direction they would go.

He glanced at his bedside clock. It was half past six - not worth trying to go back to sleep but too early to get up without disturbing the rest of his family. The vision he had experienced had been very detailed but none of the images seemed at all familiar. David had spent many holidays staying with his gran but he had never ventured further than her garden or the village.

After lying on his bed and mulling over everything he had experienced for an hour, he dressed but waited until his mother had called him several times before he emerged looking as sick as he could. David's father had left early so he focused all his attention on convincing his mother that he was far too ill to go to school. However she steadfastly saw straight through his ploy.

At the point he was about to give up, something very strange happened. He could hear someone crying and sobbing. It took him a couple of bewildered minutes to realise it was him. But why? Why was he crying? Through his tears he caught a glimpse of his mother's face, obviously distressed, as she hurried to comfort him. As she held him in her arms, it came to him. These were not tears of sadness, they were of joy. Ryan's face appeared in his mind joined by that of another - Ryan's father, the man from the hospital bed. He must have arrived home. The timing could not have been better. As his mother wiped his eyes with her apron, she said the words he had been waiting for.

"I really think perhaps you should stay home today and get some rest. I have to work up at the manor, but I will ask Millie to check on you throughout the morning and I will be home about four thirty."

David hiccupped, "It's okay" and reassured her that he would be alright. "I am just a bit tired that's all."

With that he slowly made his way out of the kitchen and back upstairs to his bedroom. David felt a little bad about deceiving his mother, but needs must. The morning passed painfully slowly. Millie popped her head around the door a couple of times - the last time to say that she was going to the shops and taking Joe with her and asked him to keep an ear open for his gran in case she needed anything.

As soon as he heard the door close he made his way down the stairs, pausing at the hall table to dial Susan's number. He breathed a sigh of relief as she answered.

"Is it all clear?" he asked Susan.

"Well she has been up and about this morning but she has gone back to bed so we should be okay."

Stopping to catch his breath every now and again, David ran as much of the way to the old manse as he could. The sun was shining faintly. David found Susan sitting on the front porch with the two books in her lap.

"Please, please tell me you have found something helpful", begged David. "We are running out of time", he added as he climbed the front steps.

"Well up until now, no", she replied. "But the chapter I have just started talks about what happens when two stones are set into conflict with each other. It is slow going I am afraid, but I am reading as fast as I can."

"Can you keep going if I tell you about something?"

"Yes, I think so", Susan replied.

"Well I had another vision last night, while I was sleeping."

He went on to describe it, only stopping when Susan wanted to question him about certain facts. When he had finished, he sat quietly waiting for her to finish the chapter she was reading.

Finally she looked up from the book and said in quite a matter of fact way: "Well this can't be ignored although there is nothing in your dream that can help us at the moment. I have no doubt that when the time is right, everything will make sense. I am sure at the time your gran included all the information she could in this book. But it is hard to see what use it can be to us at the moment. Do you remember the type of stone that Madam Serina had in her ring?"

"I am sure it was a garnet," David replied and added, "It was large and very dark."

"Well, in that case assuming she has had the stone for many years, we are in trouble. Garnets, although not as powerful as some other stones, strengthen with age. If in possession of someone with a strong and highly developed gift, they can be almost impossible to overpower. Your sapphire is one of the purest stones but you have not had it that long and so far we don't know how powerful you are. With your gifts changing we must assume your power is increasing but to what level?"

As Susan finished speaking she leaned backwards with a defeated sigh. David sat looking at her. Susan was such a good friend. Although she had only been part of his life for a short time, she had accepted him without prejudice and never questioning his strangeness. Here they were, sitting so calmly and discussing rationally things he would normally hesitate to speak about. He made a mental note that one day he would find a way to repay this huge debt he felt he owed her. He was determined to be the friend she deserved.

Focusing once again on the situation, he asked, "Have there been any cases of clashes of power of this kind, and if so what was the outcome? Which stones are the most powerful and how did their strength affect things?"

"It all does clearly come down to power and who and which stone has the most. In the majority of cases the person who is overpowered is left in some kind of weakened state. Their gemstone is irreparably damaged. Some have even died as their stone disintegrated. It seems there have been cases where both parties were so evenly matched that they were both destroyed."

After a few moments of absolute silence, Susan stated, "Your power must come from the fortunetellers' category. There must be some way of testing your abilities."

With that she picked up the book with new vigour. "Try something for me. Tell me my future. Concentrate and give me an idea of what you can see."

As David was about to say he could not because her barrier would prevent him, a vision flooded his mind and music and the chatter of many voices surrounded him. At first he did not recognise the scene, but as he turned he found himself once again looking out through a pair of French doors. As before Susan was present, her hair in ribbons and wearing a pretty dress. Once again the dark-haired boy appeared by her side and reaching down to kiss Susan, he looked up to catch David's eye and wink at him. This jolted David back to reality.

Susan looked at him expectantly. "Well?" she prompted.

David described the party to her without mentioning the boy. There was a nagging thought buzzing in his head. He had the strangest feeling. Never before had he experienced someone interacting with him during a vision. He told himself he was just being paranoid, that the boy was probably winking at someone else in the room. Not convinced, he turned his attention back to Susan.

"That's fine as far as it goes," said Susan. "But it won't help us much as we have no idea when this will happen. Do you have any sense how far in the future this might be?"

David, feeling deflated, shook his head.

"You have been practising haven't you?" David asked Susan. "Did you find lowering your barrier much easier this time?"

"Yes," admitted Susan with a smile. "At first I was afraid to but realised that there is no time for that. There is too much at stake. The incident with you made me realise that I was hiding behind this barrier instead of being able to control it. Practice really does make perfect and on that note we must start building your defences up too."

"I know I must," answered David. "But at the moment, I don't feel it's a priority."

Glancing at his watch he realised that if he wanted to be home before his mother, he would have to leave in five minutes. Gathering his thoughts, he asked Susan to try and find the answers to certain questions - were there any descriptions of powerful fortunetellers, what could they do and how a duel between powerful characters worked?

With his mind racing, the journey home was a blur. Millie was in the garden playing with Joe. She did not notice David slip quietly up the front path and into the house. Something had been playing on his mind for some time and he felt that he could not leave it any longer. Susan was on the front line yet she had no protection at all. Yes, she could stop people from reading her mind but that would not stop Madam Serina from draining her life force if their paths were to cross. David knew from his gran that amber protected against magical attacks. As it was too risky to try and connect with his gran at the moment, he would have to go through her jewellery box himself in search of something suitable. The box was, as usual, on his gran's dressing table. He felt uneasy about delving in her belongings but he felt sure she would understand and even approve.

The box was very full and had many different compartments. Eventually he found what he was looking for. It came in the form of a charm bracelet - each charm had a piece of amber embedded in it. As he held the bracelet in his hands he felt a warm wave of relief. He had to give it to Susan as soon as possible and make her promise never to be without it.

When his mother popped her head around the bedroom door she found David sitting on his bed reading. "You look much brighter," she said. "Did you manage to sleep at all?"

"Not really," answered David. This was nearly the truth. "But I do feel a lot more rested. I am sure that I will be fine for school in the morning." Susan had said that Aunt Joan was insisting she went back to school tomorrow so he knew that he would not have to face being there without her.

Chapter 12

DRY RUN

As David collapsed into the seat next to Susan on the bus the next morning, all he wanted to do was present her with the bracelet but to do so in front of all his school companions was not a good idea. They made stilted, polite conversation, waiting until they could be alone. Susan was overwhelmed with the gift of the charm bracelet, especially when he explained the protective power of amber.

Then her smile faded. "I feel like I have let you down," she whispered.

David looked at her questioningly.

"I haven't been able to find anything to help us," she said in a rush. "I keep looking but none of the information I have read suggests that there is any way that someone, as new to their gifts as you are, can overpower such an experienced menace. There have been cases where two or three united people have managed it but you do not have anyone else to support you. If only your gran was still fully with us, if you know what I mean?"

David reached over and gently touched her arm. "It's okay. I know you are doing your best. If the information is not there, you cannot find it. But I will find a way. Gran told me that this is my fight and I must face it whatever the consequences."

Susan looked horrified. "You are not Harry Potter you know. There is no magical force protecting you from this evil creature. If you duel using your minds and gifts and she wins, you could be left mentally impaired or, even worse, dead."

"We need to know more," David countered. "And I am starting to believe that it is not going to be found within that book. The fair arrives tomorrow. We need to go and do some reconnaissance work. After school I will go and see the lie of the land. It would be great if you could come but I will understand if you're not keen to do so."

Susan was offended. "As if I would let you go on your own. But what do you hope to find? She is bound to be at her strongest there with so many people at her command."

"I hope," David stated firmly, "that she will not see this coming. She will underestimate us and her guard will be down."

"That's rather a lot to hope for," Susan remarked. "Oh

Dry Run

no! Have you seen the time. We are late for registration and you know how fussy Miss Brightman can be."

Their form tutor gave them a very stern look as they sheepishly entered the form room. Luckily for them she was distracted by questioning the class about the whereabouts of Ryan Walsh. This was the second day he had been absent. David was going to put his hand up and explain but decided better of it. He did not wish to draw attention to himself and anyway, how would he explain how he knew? Just then Jill Smith, the butcher's daughter, who hung around with Ryan, stood up and handed Miss Brightman a letter which explained that because Ryan's father had returned home after a long absence, the family were spending some quality time together.

Every spare moment they had, David and Susan went through different scenarios that might help them gain the information they needed. There were so many unknowns. Susan had discovered that Madam Serina's power had originated from her healing gift but she had used the gift solely for her own benefit by using other people's energy to not only heal herself but to stop and reverse herself ageing. There were no other accounts of her gift but that did not mean that they should not be ready for all eventualities. By the end of the day, they had drawn up a basic plan. The only thing that they knew for certain was that they must avoid an out and out conflict for as long as possible.

David walked up the lane to his house. Having put on a brave face for Susan, he was now feeling a little exhausted and anxious. The information she had given him pointed strongly to the difficulty of defeating Madam Serina. Yet in his mind he knew that he must try and that all hope was not yet lost. As usual he found his mother in the kitchen. His father was also home. He poured himself a drink of juice from the fridge and sat down next to his father.

"Good day at school son?" his dad asked.

"Just the usual," he lied.

Mr Trent glanced at his wife in a questioning way. She made her way to the table and sat before addressing David. "Things have been a little strange around here recently. What with Jessica being away, the family seems a bit disoriented but your father and I think a family night out at the fair will help bring us together. We spoke to your sister but she feels she is too far behind with her schoolwork to make it. She promises she will be home as soon as she has caught up."

David decided it was time to resurrect his brave face and produced what he hoped was a convincing smile. If his parents did not believe him they showed no evidence of it. Putting on a brave front was fine but it was also tiring, so he made his excuses after dinner and went to his bedroom. He quickly worked his way through his homework. It was an inadequate job but at that moment he felt his priorities were elsewhere.

Sleep would not come and his mind started to wander. Different people and their future happiness popped in and out of his mind - Ryan and his father enjoying a day out, his sister having a pillow fight with her best friend and, most surprisingly, Millie enjoying a kiss with the mechanic who worked at the local garage.

Suddenly he found himself running. He felt like his chest would burst. It was the same dream with more details this time but still it made little sense. His pursuer was still unknown. The location still evaded him. Yet the end was the same - hiding up the rope ladder gave him a wonderful feeling of safety.

When the dream ended, he stayed in a kind of sleep-like state seeing faces drifting in and out of focus. His mind was desperately trying to tie things together. At home his sister was quiet and moody, yet the images he had seen of Jessica seemed really happy. His gran's book held so much information, but they could not find the answers they needed. His own gifts were increasing day by day, but his control of them was still erratic at best. Yes he could bring forth images of people, just not the right ones to make a difference.

It was a relief when morning finally arrived. Although he had had the opportunity to rest, his body as well as his brain felt exhausted. Everything was an effort. By the time he joined Susan on the bus, all he wanted to do was close his eyes. On closer inspection Susan was not looking her best either and David guessed that she had also not had a good night's sleep.

He felt a hand on his shoulder. Slowly turning his head, he was alarmed to find Ryan smiling at him. Surely it was a trick and any minute he would get a cuff round the head or a thump in his midriff. He braced himself only to be shocked when Ryan lent closer and whispered "Thanks" in his ear before smiling and returning to his seat. Susan who had overheard looked questioningly at him and scowled when he just shrugged his shoulders without giving her an explanation.

The day seemed to crawl along interminably. They tried with difficulty to concentrate on their lessons. Attempting to block other people's thoughts did not stop his own from screaming inside his head. By lunchtime David felt his head would simply explode. Susan started teaching him how to block intrusive thoughts more effectively. After they had eaten, Susan and David found a quiet spot in one of the empty classrooms. It was raining heavily outside so their chance of being alone for long was not great.

At first it seemed hopeless. There was still too much noise and when Susan backed away it became progressively worse.

"You must find something to focus on. One thing only, David," she sighed impatiently.

David tried desperately to do as she asked but the only thing that kept popping into his mind was the image in his vision of Susan being kissed by the dark-haired winking boy. Suddenly he became aware of a lull in the background noise. It was such a relief he nearly missed Susan calling his name. When her face came back into focus she was smiling, "You did it! That's great. Now you need to become aware of the time it has taken you." She pointed at the clock on the wall and David was shocked to see forty five minutes had passed.

Focusing on something in a quiet classroom was one thing: it proved to be much more difficult to block out thoughts when there were lots of other people about. Science was the first lesson after lunch and with the stress of their forthcoming plan and David's inability to focus his thoughts for more than a few moments, it was going to be a long and demanding afternoon. For a time, while engrossed in his experiment, David felt at peace only to be disturbed by someone tapping on his shoulder. It was Ryan. As David turned to face him, David immediately noticed the change in Ryan's aura. Instead of the dark pulsating mass it had been for a long time, there was a pure green light - like sunlight penetrating through a tender summer leaf. It even glowed warmly. David registered the difference in Ryan's voice - it seemed softer and more sincere than he would have thought possible.

"I don't know how you knew," Ryan said with a smile. "And quite frankly I don't care. Thanks, David. I know we haven't got on very well in the past, but I would like to change that. If there is anything I can do for you. Anything.

Any time - just ask me." Then he was gone. David felt strengthened by Ryan's statement of kindness.

Thinking of what Ryan had said, David managed to complete all his experiments and even received a commendation for his work. It seemed a very strange thing to be praised for, doing well in a science lesson, as he usually struggled with this subject. He hoped that the teacher would not expect such a good achievement from him every time.

By the time the end of the school day arrived, David felt exhausted, mentally and physically. He guessed Susan was feeling the same. Unlike her normally placid self, she was short-tempered and had snapped at him twice before they had even walked to the bus.

Eventually, having regained her usual air of calmness, Susan told David where the fair was being set up. It would mean getting off the bus two stops earlier than normal - then a short walk.

The bus drove away leaving them standing alone in the country lane. Neither of them said anything or even made an attempt to move for a full five minutes. Eventually with just a quick glance at each other they set off. There was no turning back. David knew whatever the outcome, they were doing the right thing even if they did not yet know what it was.

Chapter 13

FACE TO FACE

David was not familiar with this side of the village. He was aware that his mother travelled this way to work every day, but that was of little help to them just at the moment as she was unaware of what was going on or where they were. Susan appeared completely confident as she walked along in a very purposeful manner.

They rounded a corner. The scene was set. All manner of tents and fun rides were being erected. There was a general hum of activity. The two friends slipped through a gateway seemingly unnoticed. There were so many people hurrying about that at first it seemed an impossible task to find Madam Serina's tent without being spotted. As they moved between items of machinery it became obvious that everyone was so busy that they were either unaware or just didn't care if other people were coming and going on the fairground. Susan and David stopped being so cautious and began to relax a little while feeling they could take a few risks.

The field in which the fair was situated was large and flat.

David started to head off around the side of a large bumper car attraction when Susan suddenly grabbed his arm. Without a word, she pointed to a large sign which read:

"LET MADAM SERINA GIVE YOU THE ANSWERS YOU ARE LOOKING FOR. CROSS HER PALM WITH SILVER AND SHE WILL USE HER INCREDIBLE GIFT TO SEE INTO YOUR FUTURE"

There was an arrow pointing away from the main part of the fair. David considerately started to ask Susan if she still wanted to be part of the plan. However the scowl she gave him made David quickly think better of continuing his question and they headed in the direction indicated by the arrow.

They found the fortuneteller's tent to the side of a large caravan. It was not an old traditional one as you would expect but a sleek modern RV model.

David turned to Susan. "You know what to do?" She nodded. As he made his way towards the tent, his legs felt like jelly. He reached out and pulled back the flaps of the tent. It was dark inside and it took his eyes some time to adjust. The scene laid out in front of him was just as you would expect - a small round table covered in a crocheted tablecloth with a crystal ball in the centre. As he stepped through the entrance and made his way towards the table, he initially sensed that he was alone. Then a familiar crooning voice said, "Come in my dear. I was wondering how long it would be before you would come and face me."

With that a curtain at the back of the tent parted and Madam Serina made her entrance. As she moved closer to the table her face came into focus. David had expected some kind of rejuvenation but was still taken aback. The woman standing in front of him looked ten years younger than when he had seen her last.

"Amazing isn't it? This visit has been so good for me, especially since meeting your dear mother." With this her eyes flashed and she laughed loudly as she said, "I had heard that your grandmother was powerful once but I never dreamt that her family would be my escape. When I have drained the life and energy from you and your family, I will be young again. I have hidden with this band of miscreants for fear of being discovered. At last I will be free."

"You know I will never let that happen," David bellowed in a voice that sounded stronger and bolder than he felt.

"Just how do you think you are going to stop me, boy?"

she spat at him. "Your gift will be great one day but I am afraid you won't be around long enough for it to mature."

With that, David felt a deep burning sensation in his chest and knew, without doubt, that she was reaching out with her power assessing his strength. Susan's timely entry at that moment was just the distraction David needed.

"Argh!" Madam Serina screamed shrilly. "How dare you bring that unnatural creature here. I don't need to read her mind to make out her little secrets. I had a visit from that frozen old aunt of yours, girl. I know all about the sad loss of your parents and your aunt having to face the future alone."

David glanced across at Susan. If Madam Serina's words were having an effect, you would never have known - Susan looked as cool as a cucumber. The rage on the fortuneteller's face was plain to see.

"I told your aunt that she would die old and alone."

"Well, that's a lie!" David exclaimed. "I have seen her future and a wedding will be taking place not too long from now."

"How dare you disagree with me," shrieked the woman. "You will soon find out that not all visions come true, you silly boy. Especially when you are not around to influence future events. But that's enough of this stupid talk. It's time for action. You first my dear." She turned to face Susan.

There was a pause. "Oh, aren't we clever?" she sneered. "Well, it will take a lot more than some amber to save you."

With that she screeched out a man's name. "Olof. Come in here. Now!"

The curtain parted and before them stood the largest, most muscle-bound man David had ever seen. But before he could feel intimidated by the newcomer's size and apparent strength, David could sense that there was something wrong with his aura. For a man of his size and strength it should have been unmistakable and well defined but instead it was transparent and he had a blank look in his eyes.

"Don't just stand there, Olof. Get them," roared Madam Serina as the giant lumbered clumsily forward.

David turned and grabbing Susan's arm, he dragged her out of the tent. At first they ran blindly away from the tent. Gradually David became aware of a sense of déjà vu - the long grass under his feet, the weak sunlight in his eyes. All of a sudden it came to him - the vision. As the seconds passed, he allowed his feet to carry him along. He was aware that

Susan was just behind him and it was all just as it should be. Trees loomed up in front of them.

"Follow me," he shouted - and darted further into the wood. The path was just as he remembered. He jumped a log and swerved into the undergrowth. Pausing momentarily in front of a large oak, he guided Susan around the trunk to the rope ladder.

"How did you ..... ?" she started to ask.

David shushed her by putting an index finger to his lips. "Oh and don't use the third rung. It will break."

Susan scrambled up the ladder and David quickly followed. The sound of their pursuer crashing about in the woodland undergrowth warned them that Olof was not far away and that knowledge sped them on.

Once they were safely inside the tree house, they both sat in silence, hardly daring to breathe. David found a small window from which he could see the man. The nearer he approached, the slower and less focused he became until finally he came to a stumbling halt about two metres away from the tree they were hiding in. He stood shaking his head as if trying to clear away some kind of confusion.

"Look," David whispered. "The further he goes, the

weaker her hold over him becomes."

Finally Olof turned and shambled back the way he came.

Waiting until all sound of him was gone, David suggested they should be getting home as time was passing and people would be wondering where they were. Luckily, from the height of their hiding place, they could make out the village and which direction they should head in. Susan's house was nearest so David said he would like to see her home. As much as this was true, David also had an ulterior motive.

Whilst hiding in the tree house, it had dawned on him how vulnerable Susan was. Yes, the amber had done its job, but if that man had caught up with her, it would not have been enough to protect her from him. There was only one thing for it. David realised that if he spoke to her about it, she would be offended and persuade him otherwise so he had to come up with a plan. Susan was not going to be happy but he considered that her safety was all that mattered.

On the corner of the street leading to The Manse, they paused to make themselves presentable and to agree a story that would account for where they had been after school instead of returning home as usual. After removing twigs and bits of cobweb from their hair and clothes, they made their way down the street and up the front steps. As they reached the top step the front door flew open and a very angry-looking Aunt Joan marched out and demanded an explanation. David waited quietly while Susan recounted the tale they had practised. As he saw Joan's face begin to soften, he knew it was now or never.

Taking a deep breath and looking straight at Aunt Joan, he demanded, "Why do you do that? Why do you push people away?"

"David!" exclaimed Susan with a shocked look on her face. But he carried on regardless.

"All your life you have moaned about wanting and needing someone. But whenever you are shown any love or affection, you push it away."

He could see what he was saying was having an effect. He just had a bit more to say, however blunt it might seem and however rudely he came across.

"If you just opened your eyes and looked outside your door, the man you have been looking for is right there."

That was the final straw. Joan turned bright red. She looked as if steam could come out of her ears at any moment. She grabbed a stunned Susan by the arm and dragged her into the house shouting, "You are never to have anything to do with that awful boy again" and slammed the door.

Chapter 14

SHOWDOWN

David made his way home with leaden steps. Although he knew he had done the right thing, his unease was lying heavily on his shoulders. Forcing himself to focus on what needed doing, he realised that if he was going to stand any chance of dealing with Madam Serina he would first have to lure Olof out of the way.

The only person he could think of asking to help him without question was Ryan. It was a long shot, but he had to try. As he reached the garden gate, his mental list of things to tackle seemed very daunting. "Take one thing at a time," he told himself.

The gargoyles, on the front path, seemed to be standing to attention. He passed them but instead of heading up the path towards the house, he walked along the hedge line to the area where the apple tree had fallen. The man who had sawn up the tree had also cut and laid the beech hedge in the traditional way used in the southwest of England, to fill the gap and make it stock-proof. David inspected his job. The hedge was much lower now but no gap was apparent, so he hoped that its protective power had been restored. Turning across the garden he entered the house by the back door. The house seemed unusually quiet. Reading a note that his mother had left on the kitchen table, he learned that they had gone to Sainsbury's to do the weekly shop and would be back later.

David sighed with relief. This window of opportunity would provide him the time to ring Ryan at his home and ask if he was prepared to help. As the phone at the other end rang, he could not, for the life of him, think what he would say.

"Lower Hamdon 456," a man's voice answered.

"H - hello," stuttered David. "C - could I speak to Ryan please?"

"Ryan!" He heard the man shout. "Phone for you."

An out of breath Ryan gasped, "Hi." He didn't seem perturbed that David was on the line. When David finished explaining his tricky situation, Ryan simply said, "Fine. Of course I could do that. What time?"

Stunned, David replaced the receiver. He never expected his request for such assistance to be unchallenged. He made his way to the bathroom and splashed his face with cold water. He must stay positive. Looking in the mirror, he tried to focus all his attention on Jessica. He needed to know she was alright. He was able to visualise her. She was reading a magazine. Although everything on the surface seemed fine, he had the feeling that something was not quite right. He couldn't put his finger on it.

The opening of the front door brought him sharply back to the present. He headed to the kitchen to greet everyone. Whilst helping his parents with unpacking the grocery bags, he managed to surreptitiously check that his father was still wearing his amber ring - another tick on the list.

"What's the plan for tomorrow evening?" he asked his mother.

"Well, dear," she replied. "Millie assured me that she will come in and sit with your gran. I know it is going to be a late night but we have decided to take Joe with us. As we mentioned before, Jessica doesn't think she can make it, but the rest of us plan to go to the fair about seven thirty."

"Sounds great," David replied. His stomach started to churn with anxiety. What had he let himself in for and how could he ensure that his family would be safe? So far, Madam

Serina hadn't given much away. He would have to slip away from his parents and try and deal with her before she had a chance to take matters into her own hands.

Not even his family's good mood could cheer David up. He made his excuses and headed miserably to his bedroom. Halfway along the landing he felt strongly drawn to his gran's room. Her door was ajar. He entered reticently and walked quietly over to where she was sitting.

"I know I mustn't expect you to speak to me, but I hope you can hear me. I promise I'll try my best," he promised her in a shaky voice. "I ... I just hope it will be enough." He stayed holding her hand gently for a moment, then quietly departed.

The silence of his room was unbearable. Desperate for some distraction, David allowed himself to be bombarded by random thoughts. Images wafted in and out of his mind. At some point he must have drifted off to sleep because the next thing he knew was his mother banging on the door saying, "David, I know it is a Saturday, but I think you should get up before lunch." He rubbed his eyes and peered at the small bedside clock which showed 11.45. He must have forgotten to set the alarm last night. As his head started to clear, it all came back to him - what day it was and all that potentially lay ahead.

Forcing down his breakfast, he felt the urgent need to speak to Susan. However this was not an option. He looked around. His father was reading the paper. His mother was feeding Joe, who as usual was fascinated by Mungo's long swishing tail which kept appearing and disappearing from under Joe's chair. David was heartened to see the cat was still present. He felt reassured by the protection Mungo provided the family ensuring that they were safe within their home. One couldn't be too careful.

Time, like grains of sand, was running through his hands. So as not to raise suspicion and be questioned by his parents, he sat in the sitting room pretending to watch television whilst focusing on his gemstone with all his power of concentration. He knew he could harness great energy if only he could find how to tap into it. Even the old fortuneteller herself had said so. But how could he possibly achieve this in the little time available?

The more he focused, the less effective he seemed. The day passed with constant interruptions. People came and went. In the late afternoon, David answered the door for what seemed like the umpteenth time. It was Fred Dingle, the postman. He was a regular visitor to the house. Fred often stayed talking to Mrs Trent for several hours. David showed him into the kitchen where his mother was ironing her best blouse to wear at the fair that evening.

"I won't keep you long," David heard him say. "I know we have been discussing my future at great length but I wanted to tell you that I haven't the courage to go ahead with it."

"Oh Fred!" his mother exclaimed impatiently. "Faint heart never won fair maiden. This really has gone on long enough."

David's head swam. So that's whose future wedding celebrations he had been allowed to glimpse. The vision hit him again like a replay. He found himself once again at the party but, instead of the previous images, he saw Fred and Aunt Joan holding hands - the diamond of her engagement ring and the gold of her wedding ring sparkling and glinting in the light.

Without a doubt, David knew he had to convince Fred to ask Joan to be his wife. He waited by the front door and cornered Fred as he tried to leave. "You must do it!" David hissed forcibly, quite unlike his usual self. "My mother has been too patient with you. I think you need a kick up the backside. You came to this family because you know we can help. You have to believe me when I say that you, Fred Dingle, and Joan Roberts are meant to be together. If you can sum up enough courage to propose, she will accept."

Fred gawped - his eyes bulging like those of a rabbit frozen in car headlights. Once he had managed to overcome his shock at being spoken to in such a startling and rude way by Mrs Trent's normally polite and even-tempered son, he pushed his shoulders back and stated resolutely, "I will. I will - first thing on Monday morning. Now if you will excuse me, I must hurry. I must reach the jeweller's shop in Braunton before they close." With that he was gone.

Feeling pleased that he had helped secure Fred and Joan's future happiness, David felt more positive about this evening's plan. Before he knew it, it was 7pm and time to get ready. What did one wear to confront an adversary in a deathly clash of minds? Trying to keep a sense of humour - however black the situation - he supposed that if he was defeated, he would no longer be around to care. Nonchalantly, he changed into an old pair of jeans and a warm jumper. The nights were drawing in and it might be cold later.

Before the family left the house, David carried out a last minute check. Mungo was contentedly asleep on a padded kitchen chair, all the downstairs windows were shut tight and Millie was wearing the clean overall which had been left out for her. (Earlier in the day he had found a beautiful amber brooch and clipped it to the inside of the pocket. He couldn't think how else he could provide her with protection without a tricky and detailed explanation and there was no time for that.)

Mr Trent decided that, as it was a dry night, they should walk to the fair. It would only take fifteen minutes. They would take Joe's pushchair as it was too far for him to walk. The stroll there and back would do them good and the hassle of parking their car in a field with hundreds of others would be avoided. As he closed the garden gate, David paused to take a good look at the house that felt like home even a short time after they had moved in, just in case things didn't go his way. He shuddered.

The light was gently fading as they walked along the quiet lanes. It wasn't long before the sound of fairground music could be heard. With every step they took, the music became louder. Soon they were assailed by the smell of diesel engines, candyfloss and fried onions. As they rounded the last corner and the fair came into view, David was struck by how strange the sight of the fair was stretched out before him. It seemed as if he was seeing everything rolling out in front of him in a series of time-lapse frames playing at a three quarter speed. The whole site seemed to be enveloped in a large softly swirling grey cloud. He took a hurried look to see if the rest of his family had noticed and was shocked to see how blurred they appeared. Sensing this was his chance to escape, he glanced quickly at them and slipped away.

His first priority was to remove the fortuneteller's sign. The last thing he needed was innocent bystanders becoming embroiled in the clash or hurt. David easily located the sign and made short work of uprooting it from the ground. He tossed it into the back of the nearest lorry. He glanced at his watch. It was nearly 8.00. If everything was going according to plan, Ryan should be very busy about now. David made his way to the edge of the tent. He could hear a sickly sweet crooning voice informing someone that they were due to come into some money..... a lot of money. "Let me hold your hand for a moment and I may be able to tell you some more…"

As David peered through a gap in the tent's lining, he saw his form tutor, Miss Brightman, reaching out her left hand. He wanted to rush immediately into the tent and protect her, but he knew he must bide his time. Just a few more moments should be enough - if Ryan had been successful!

He could hardly watch as his favourite teacher's aura faded before his very eyes. By the time the old fortuneteller had released her hand, Miss Brightman's aura was almost transparent. Horrified, David watched her leave in a somnambulant state as she stumbled out of the tent without a word.

"Like moths to a flame and just as helpless," David heard the old woman cackle to herself. As David made to enter the tent, his watch beeping the hour alerted Madam Serina. She swung round to face him as he entered. She had a devilishly delighted look on her face.

"Come in. Sit down, and let me tell you your future," she trilled. "Oh that's right, you won't have one after tonight will you?"

"Well you may assume that's true," David said calmly.

"But that's not the way I see it. You may manage to turn back the clock a little by stealing life energy from people you trick with your evil ploys, but you're still ugly and old on the inside. If there's any way I can stop you, be sure I will."

"Little boy, your time has run out!" she laughed smugly. "You came here with nothing. Do you think I just wandered here with the fair by chance? Oh no! I have been planning this for months - the attack on your gran; the lightning strike on your apple tree; preventing interested purchasers from buying the house - I called in a lot of favours to make these things happen and more. Tonight, I will reap my reward. It will be like taking sweets from a baby. Now, let's not make this any harder than it should be. Why don't you just give me your hand and I promise it will be painless and over before you know it."

"Not a chance!" David retorted. "I will fight you every step of the way."

"Very well," she shouted, slamming her hands down on the table. David felt his sapphire pendant heat and throb on his skin. With all his might, he tried to mentally repel her and for a moment he thought he was making headway. He saw her smile drop. Then she renewed her efforts and he started to feel overwhelmed. Great pain filled his head. There had to be something else he could do but all he could think about was getting away from her. He started to back towards the door and then came the moment he had been dreading.

"Olof!" The fortuneteller yelled frantically for her henchman. David's heart beat rapidly against his ribcage. Had Ryan managed to stick to the plan and somehow lure the giant man away? If not, he could burst through the curtain any moment now.

No Olof appeared. David knew it was only a matter of time before he would return. He must leave now while he could. Wrenching his mind away, he turned and fled from the tent. Blindly he ran. The pain in his head was still very intense. He could hear the fortuneteller close behind him, still reaching out to tangle and duel with his mind. How long could he hold out?

Something compelled him to turn sharply to the left past the big wheel attraction. As he turned, he saw a small group of people standing right in front of him. As they came into focus, much to his surprise he saw it was his family and there holding Joe in her arms was Jessica. Even from this distance he could see that his visions of her had been inaccurate. She looked so tired - with big dark circles around her eyes. Half of him wanted to turn and lead this crazed menace away from his family, but the rest of him wanted them close.

As he skidded to a breathless halt in front of them, there was a screeching gleeful voice behind him.

"So kind of you to lead me to your family. It will save me so much time and effort finding them myself."

"What on earth is going on here?" Mr Trent stepped forward. "David why are you being pursued by this insane woman?"

Just then, there was a loud roar. David knew time was running out. Olof had returned. He was on his way to add his considerable strength and support to help Madam Serina overpower them. Courageously facing her, he backed towards his family. How could he have so stupidly led them all here to their doom?

Olof burst into sight and began lumbering towards them. "Who shall I start with first?" the woman sniggered. As David took one last step, he tripped over a tussock of grass and would have fallen to the ground if his sister had not caught him by the arm. Suddenly enlightenment came to him. How could he have not realised this before? Summoning the last of his failing strength, he turned and smiled tremulously at Jessica.

"Glad you could make it," he gasped. "Take my hand." His right hand met Jessica's. His left reached across to Joe. As they formed a circuit and contact was made between the three siblings, streams of coloured light exploded around them like a firework display on the 5th of November. Searing flashes - so bright you couldn't look at them without wincing - of blue, red and white merged together then burst forth and, as one, hit their attacker square in the chest. For a moment the evil menace withstood the force, but then she let out a hideous blood-curdling scream and collapsed to her knees.

The lights vanished as quickly as they had appeared and as they did so, the sight in front of David changed as if someone had pressed a fast forward button. The lights of the fairground were brighter, the music louder and the grey cloud seemed to melt away. Only a few metres away Olof stood, like a waxwork. David walked towards him and rested a hand on his shoulder. "It's okay," he said softly. The giant man turned his head and gazed blankly at him.

David turned to tell his family he thought it was time to

go home, only to be faced by Madam Serina. She was trembling violently and struggling to breathe and speak.

"You....will ....regret....this!" she rasped out word by word. "When I tell the others what you have done, they will avenge me and restore my powers."

Then before his very eyes she seemed to age, at first looking ten years older, then twenty, then thirty. He could tell by her diminishing aura that her power was failing rapidly. When she was completely debilitated and posed no further threat, he confidently walked past her and spoke authoritatively to his family.

"I'm just going to help this poor man, and then I think we should go home."

Without speaking, his family turned as one and followed him across the fairground. As they passed the very old and incapacitated woman, David couldn't help saying, "Didn't you see that coming? Call yourself a fortuneteller?" She spat weakly at him.

Chapter 15

UNITED AT LAST

David escorted the giant man back to the centre of the fairground, where he left him in the company of the friendly woman running the coconut shy. He and his family then made their way soberly across the field and out into the lane. It took a few moments for their eyes to adjust to the dark, but it was a clear night and a full moon lit the way. The family walked along in silence for which David was glad. There was so much to take in. The things he had seen and felt. What had really happened?

He glanced sideways at his sister. The moon was shining on her face and she looked relaxed. It was hard to believe what she had been through earlier. As soon as he had been shown the way and reached out to her and his brother, they had immediately connected - their minds and gifts shared evenly between them, forming an indestructible unit.

Initially Jessica had been experiencing the dark side of her gift. Like David she also experienced visions, but hers were of people's sadness and grief and the tragedies that might befall them. No wonder her mood swings had been so bad. Why, David wondered, had their gran never spoken to either of them about it? Joe, on the other hand, being so much younger, was merely channelled into his surroundings. He didn't, as yet, have to deal with other people's emotions whether happy or sad. He was simply in tune with the mice scurrying around searching for food, bats sweeping through the dark sky catching fluttering moths and barn owls hunting silently for prey. However, David was aware that tonight his sister and brother had experienced the same range of emotions as he had at the fair. They shared the same connection. It was going to be a long night. Apart from Joe, there would be no sleep for anyone until what had taken place had been discussed fully - and if possible explained and understood.

The lights, glowing warmly from the old cottage windows, looked so welcoming, but the whole family paused outside the front door. They were all aware that once the door had been opened and everything revealed, life might never be the same again.

Millie must have heard them approaching and it was she who inadvertently broke the spell which had frozen them in uncertainty on the front step. As light burst forth from the opening door, her beaming smile re-animated them and they piled into the hallway, removing their coats and shoes as one.

"Well," said Mr Trent.

"Well, I think we are all overdue a family meeting," David and Jessica declared simultaneously.

He smiled reassuringly and simply answered, "Quite."

Mrs Trent thanked Millie for taking care of her mother during their outing to the fair and, wishing her goodnight, subtly manoeuvred her through the open door. As she closed it, she asked, "Cocoa all round then?"

"I'll fetch Gran," said David, and before anyone could stop him he bounded up the stairs. Five minutes later, he returned sedately to the kitchen with her clinging to his arm. Everyone sat around the table waiting for them. He made Gran comfortable, took a deep breath and addressed his family.

"I hope I can explain everything. I'm sure tonight must have come as a huge surprise, but it has been building for some time. It all started with Gran and I think it would only be right that we should finish this evening with her included in the family meeting."

"That's a very sweet idea," Mrs Trent acknowledged. "But I hardly think she is up to it."

David remained steadfast. "Could you all hold hands?" he asked while picking up his gran's left hand and motioned for Jessica to do the same with her right. His parents looked sceptical, but did as they were bid, with Joe sitting on Mrs Trent's lap.

David turned to his sister and instructed, "Focus on Gran and the fact you would like to communicate with her." He closed his eyes and reached out with his mind.

Mrs Trent did the same and gasped. "Mum, is that really you?"

A faint voice replied, "Yes, my dear girl, it is. Listen very carefully, for our time is short and this will be the last time I will be able to speak to you all.

"Mathew. You have turned out to be the best son-in-law I could have wished for. I can see that tonight has been a shock but the chat we had, when you asked for Jill's hand in marriage, should have prepared you for this a little.

"Jill, my darling daughter, you made it clear to me many years ago that you would not or could not accept your gift and I never pushed you. But your children must make their own choices and I hope you can support them whatever they choose to do.

"My special, special grandchildren. I am so proud of you all. Jessica, the road you have travelled has been a hard one. I know you feel out of control at times - at odds with your gift. But please, think carefully before you decide. David and Joe, I am so sorry. I never intended you to receive your stones at such a young age. But when I realised my time was running out, I had to act quickly with the little power I had left. Convincing Millie to do my bidding was not hard. She is a sweet girl with a very open mind but she must be protected, for more dangers lie ahead I fear.

"Well, there is nothing left but to say that I love you all, and although I will not be able to communicate with you in this way again, know that I am watching over you always."

Having uttered that final sentence, she once again retreated into the shell of her previous self. Feeling that things might quickly fall apart, David filled his family in about what had been going on and how, for many years, Madam Serina had preyed on other people's life energies for her own benefit. He must have talked for at least forty minutes before Jessica interrupted.

"She has definitely gone, hasn't she? I mean, there is no way she can come back?"

"No, she has gone," David reassured her. "But with the terrible threats she made, I am afraid that there could be others like her. That is why we must tell each other everything we come across day to day and experience through visions - no matter how trivial some things might seem."

He answered the questions his parents - trying to make sense of what had taken place - posed to the best of his ability. He then wished everyone goodnight. As he was leaving the kitchen, he said, "I need you to do something for me, Jessica."

"Anything," she replied.

"Could you text Susan? I am concerned that she might not answer me. I will give you her number. Just say, 'All okay.' She must be so worried."

"No problem," his sister replied. "Sleep well."

"You know," said David, "I think I will."

Chapter 16

A BRIGHTER DAY

David slept like a log. With such a weight lifted, it really was his first good night's sleep in weeks. If it hadn't been for his mother, banging on the door to inform him that it was ten o'clock and he had a visitor, he would have slept on.

"Quick! She has some great news," his mother said excitedly. "Although I must say, she doesn't seem that happy about it."

As David dressed, he had a pretty good idea what the news was. He hoped it was not that which had made Susan unhappy. He went downstairs and found Susan in the sitting room.

"Well, I suppose you already know?"

A grin spread across David's face. "Yes, just call me Cupid," he replied.

Seeing that she didn't look at all impressed, he straightened his face and said, "Let's grab a drink and sit in the garden. I have so much to tell you."

Susan didn't reply, but followed him into the kitchen. He

poured them each a glass of orange juice which they carried outside. It was drizzling and grey, so David headed down the path to a small arbour with a seat under it.

"Let me say one thing before we start," David said hesitantly. "You are the best friend I have ever had. I know you feel I have treated you badly and made decisions concerning you without consulting you first but I had to keep you safe. I could not think of any way of protecting you if you had come to the fair. When we first visited Madam Serina, I realised how great her power was. All I could think about was if I failed to overcome her who would protect you."

He raised his eyes to meet hers, desperately hoping that she would understand. It was a relief to see that, although she didn't look happy, she was no longer angry.

"Well, are you going to tell me what happened or not?" she said.

David reclined on the bench seat and recounted the whole story detail by detail. Although she gasped at times and looked wide-eyed occasionally, she did not speak until he had finished.

"So you felt you could risk Ryan's life by asking for his

help but not mine!" she said, but he could tell by her voice that she was no longer angry with him.

"Aunt Joan and Fred Dingle!" exclaimed David to change the subject. "How do you feel about that?"

"Well, I do think you could have given us some warning," responded Susan. "I know you've been busy, but can you imagine my poor aunt's face when she opened the door to the postman on a Sunday and there he was on one knee, holding out a diamond ring instead of a letter before proposing to her. And, oh my goodness I was so surprised when she accepted his proposal. Then when they started kissing in the kitchen, I couldn't get out of there fast enough. Eugh, old people kissing. It's not normal."

David grinned. "Something tells me you had better start looking for a pink bridesmaid's dress."

They both laughed.

"On a more serious note though," interrupted Susan. "Do you think Madam Serina's threats are something to be concerned about?"

"That's something we will only discover in the future," David replied. "In fact, I am more worried about the present. We have dealt with the threat this time and hopefully any danger is truly over. Helping Jessica develop her gift, as well as constructively working with my own, is going to keep me busy for now. With your help of course," he added quickly.

"Do you need to ask?" she said with a smile. "Although I'm not quite so convinced about your new friend." She turned to look towards the garden gate. David made out the slight and wiry shape of Ryan.

"I know, he seems an unlikely candidate. But he was there for me as soon as I asked and that's all I need to know. I'll go and fetch him."

David's route took him past the front door where he found Jessica brooding over a cup of coffee. "It will be okay. I'll help you, you know," David reassured her.

"I know you will," she replied gratefully. "But it's not just me who needs your help." He looked questioningly at her. "Your new friend," she continued. "There's a darkness around him. I can't make it out, but sense that he's going to need your support over the next few months."

"There you see!" David remarked eagerly. "You're doing it already. You're using your gift to make a difference."

Ryan seemed embarrassed and awkward to start with, but when David invited him to join them and began chatting away, he visibly relaxed. They rejoined Susan in the arbour and mulled over what had happened.

"They have gone, you know," Ryan blurted out when Susan mentioned the fair. "I went round there this morning to return the picture that I stole from Olof to make him chase me - it was all I could think of on the spur of the moment. But there was no sign of them. They must have packed up as soon as they closed last night."

"I don't think I'll feel the same way about fairs ever again," shuddered Susan and the boys both agreed.

"One thing's for sure," stated David. "We must be more prepared next time."

"Next time!" Susan and Ryan yelled, and they all fell about laughing.

48691407R00090

Printed in Poland
by Amazon Fulfillment
Poland Sp. z o.o., Wrocław